W9-CBS-887

A Test of Faith

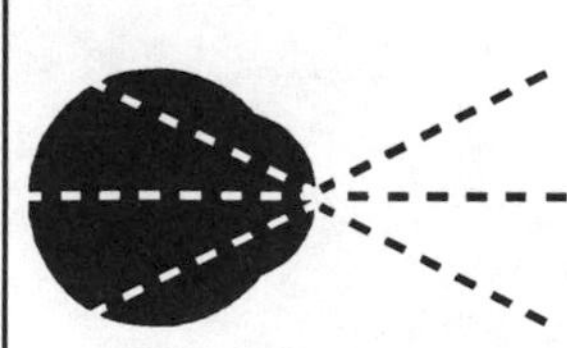

This Large Print Book carries the Seal of Approval of N.A.V.H.

MYSTERY AND THE MINISTER'S WIFE, BOOK 3

A Test of Faith

Carol Cox

THORNDIKE PRESS
A part of Gale, Cengage Learning

GALE
CENGAGE Learning™

Detroit • New York • San Francisco • New Haven, Conn • Waterville, Maine • London

Thorndike Press, a part of Gale, Cengage Learning.

Thorndike Press® Large Print Christian Mystery.
The text of this Large Print edition is unabridged.
Other aspects of the book may vary from the original edition.
Set in 16 pt. Plantin.
Printed on permanent paper.

LIBRARY OF CONGRESS CATALOGING-IN-PUBLICATION DATA

Cox, Carol.
A test of faith / by Carol Cox.
p. cm. — (Thorndike Press large print Christian mystery)
(Mystery and the minister's wife)
ISBN-13: 978-1-4104-1253-9 (alk. paper)
ISBN-10: 1-4104-1253-9 (alk. paper)
1. Spouses of clergy—Fiction. 2. Clergy—Fiction. 3. Automobile thieves—Fiction. 4. Large type books. I. Title.
PS3553.O9148T47 2009b
813'.54—dc22 2008040726

Published in 2009 by arrangement with Guideposts a Church Corporation.

Printed in the United States of America
1 2 3 4 5 6 7 12 11 10 09 08

To Emmalee, who brightened our lives by coming into the world as this book was being written.

Chapter One

Heart pounding, Kate Hanlon bolted upright and tried to figure out what had awakened her. Her eyes probed the darkness, searching for anything out of the ordinary in the dark corners of the bedroom. Nothing seemed amiss. But something had jolted her out of a sound sleep. What was it?

A loud jangling broke the silence, and Kate realized it was the telephone. Reaching across Paul's sleeping form, she scrambled for the receiver, hoping to still the ringing before it woke him.

She yanked the cordless phone off its cradle and jabbed at the Talk button in time to cut off the next ring. The bedside clock read 1:15 a.m. Kate's throat tightened. Calls that came in the middle of the night seldom meant good news.

"Please don't let anything be wrong with the kids." She breathed the prayer in a quivering whisper, then pressed the receiver against her ear. "Hello?"

"Kate? Is that you?"

The high-pitched, breathless voice on the other end of the line only heightened her concern. She shook off the last remnants of sleep and tried to keep her tone even.

"Yes, this is Kate. Who's calling, please."

"It's LuAnne Matthews. I'm callin' from the diner."

Kate's anxiety rose another notch. The Country Diner wasn't an all-night establishment, so LuAnne couldn't be waiting on tables at this hour. Nothing short of an emergency would have brought her friend down there in the middle of the night.

"What's happening? What's wrong?"

She heard LuAnne draw a shaky breath before she answered. "There's a car sittin' in the dining room."

Kate pressed the heel of her hand against her forehead and squeezed her eyes shut. She couldn't have heard correctly. Maybe she was having a bad dream. Too much paprika in last night's Hungarian beef perhaps?

"Say that again. Slowly."

"A car, Kate. It crashed through the front window, and it's sittin' smack dab in the middle of the dining room. It plowed right through the tables and chairs, and there's glass everywhere. It looks like a tornado came through here."

"Oh, good heavens!"

Paul stirred and grunted, and Kate dropped her voice to a whisper. "Is anyone hurt?"

"No, thank goodness. There weren't any customers here, of course, and Loretta and I both went home hours ago."

"What about the driver?"

"There isn't any."

"Excuse me?"

"There isn't any driver here," LuAnne repeated, enunciating each syllable with care. "No sign of him — or her — anywhere."

Images played through Kate's mind of someone wandering the streets of Copper Mill in the wee hours of the morning, injured and possibly in shock. "Whose car is it?"

"I don't know." LuAnne's voice wobbled. "I don't recognize it, and the sheriff can't tell either. The license plate's missin'."

Paul pushed himself up on one elbow and rubbed his hand over his face. "What's going on?" he murmured, his voice heavy with sleep.

"No driver and no license plate? How can

that be?" Kate cupped one hand over the mouthpiece and explained the situation to Paul. "There's been an accident down at the diner. No one's hurt, but LuAnne's terribly upset."

Kate swung her legs over the edge of the bed, flipped on the bedside lamp, and stood unsteadily. Goose bumps prickled along her arms as she padded across the carpet to the closet, mentally sorting through her wardrobe for something that would protect her against the chilly February night.

"It'll only take us a few minutes to get dressed. We'll be right down to help you clean up. Is there anything I can —"

"Oh, I'm makin' a mess of this," LuAnne cut in. "That's not why I called. There's already a passel of people down here, and the sheriff just told us we can start straightening the place up . . ."

She paused so long, Kate wondered if the connection had been broken.

"It's your wallet," LuAnne said at last. "It was lyin' on the passenger seat."

Kate's hand froze in the act of pulling a warm pair of navy slacks from their hanger. "What? That's impossible!"

Paul sat up in bed. "What's impossible?"

Kate gestured for him to wait.

"Impossible or not, there it was," LuAnne

said. "I saw it myself."

"There must be some mistake. We'll see you in a few minutes."

Paul joined Kate at the closet and reached for a pair of jeans and his favorite sweatshirt. "I'm assuming that conversation made more sense when you could hear both halves of it."

Kate warmed with gratitude at Paul's willingness to join her with no argument, and with little explanation from her. "Not really. Nothing seems to be making much sense right now."

She stepped into her slacks and pulled a thick patterned turtleneck sweater over her head, then hurried to the chair where she had left her purse before going to bed. She unzipped the center compartment and reached inside.

The air whooshed out of her lungs. "It's gone."

"What's gone?" Paul stood before the mirror, running a comb through his salt-and-pepper hair. "I'm perfectly aware we're getting ready to head down to the diner at one thirty in the morning, but it would be nice to know a little more about what's going on."

Kate zipped her purse closed and tried to still her whirling thoughts. "Someone drove a car through the diner's front window. It sounds like a disaster zone."

"And LuAnne's trying to handle it on her own? Isn't Loretta down there too?"

"I didn't ask, but I'm sure she is." Kate stepped to the dresser, picked up her brush, and ran it through her strawberry-blonde hair with a few quick strokes. "Doesn't the sheriff usually notify the business owner when something like this happens? I'd assume he contacted Loretta, and then she called LuAnne."

While LuAnne was the public face of the diner, Loretta was the devoted owner and head cook.

"So we're heading down there to be the cleanup crew? Not that I mind helping out, but I'm trying to understand why LuAnne phoned us."

Kate tossed her brush back onto the dresser and turned to face him. "No, we're going there to pick up my wallet."

A puzzled frown formed a crease between Paul's eyebrows. "You mean they found your wallet at the diner? I didn't know you'd lost it."

Unexpected tears stung Kate's eyes. "I didn't either. But that isn't the worst of it. LuAnne said it was inside the car that went through the window."

Paul wrapped his arms around her, and she leaned against him, drawing comfort from his quiet strength. "I know I had it in my purse earlier today . . . yesterday, rather. How could I have been so careless as to lose it?"

Paul cradled her head against his chest. "It may not have been your fault at all. If you lost your wallet, why would it have been found inside that car? Sounds more to me like someone may have stolen it."

Kate sniffed and tilted her head back to meet his eyes. "Somehow that doesn't make me feel any better."

"Sorry." Paul's rueful grin eased her tension a bit. He kept one arm around her shoulders while they walked out into the chilly garage. "Your car or my truck?"

"Let's take my car." Kate started toward her Honda Accord and then stumbled to a stop. She raised her hands, then let them drop against her sides. "I don't have my wallet. That means I don't have my driver's license."

"My truck, then," Paul responded before she could tear up again. He helped her into the passenger seat, then he hurried around the back of the pickup to take his place behind the wheel.

Kate stared out the window as he drove.

"That doesn't make sense either."

"What doesn't?"

"If someone stole my wallet, why wouldn't they have just taken the whole purse?"

She could see Paul's smile in the glow of the dashboard lights. "You don't have to make a mystery out of everything. Why don't we wait until we get down there? Maybe we'll find the answers then."

Kate settled back against the seat. While Paul navigated the length of Smoky Mountain Road, she went back over her day.

"I know I had it with me at the Mercantile and when I got a manicure at Betty's Beauty Parlor. I didn't open my purse while I was at Smith Street Gifts, but it was still there when I used my library card."

She knotted her hands in her lap. "I just don't understand where I could have lost it."

They turned right onto Mountain Laurel Road, then left onto Smith Street. Up ahead, lights spilled out of the diner, piercing the darkness. Paul pulled his truck against the curb, climbed out, and walked around to help Kate step down to the sidewalk.

She held his arm as they closed the distance to the diner, where a gaping hole had been ripped in the front. The flashing lights atop the black-and-white sheriff's SUV lent a note of eeriness to the scene.

They stopped at what used to be the diner's entrance and stared at the wreckage within.

"How awful," Kate murmured. "It's even worse than I imagined."

Paul wrapped his fingers around hers and nodded, grim-faced.

Inside, a contingent of people moved about like a colony of ants. Kate spotted Emma Blount and Marissa Harris sweeping shards of glass into piles while Sam Gorman and Jack Wilson stacked the remains of blue Formica-topped tables against a side wall. At the counter, Deputy Skip Spencer was dusting the cash register for fingerprints.

Kate scanned the room and pointed to one of the few booths that stood untouched. "LuAnne's over there with Loretta."

She smiled at the workers as she led the way across the room, skirting a tangled heap of blue gingham curtains that had once adorned the front windows.

LuAnne slid out of the booth and walked over to meet them. Clad in a pair of fleecy green pants and a dark gray parka, she looked lost without her white apron and order pad.

"Thanks for comin'." She accepted Kate's hug and held on tight.

Kate rubbed her hand up and down the other woman's back and felt her shiver. "Are you cold?"

The question struck Kate as foolish the moment the words left her lips. Of course LuAnne was cold. The breeze sweeping in through the gaping hole in the front of the building was enough to chill a penguin.

LuAnne pulled away and swiped at her red, swollen eyes, her woeful expression so different from her usual cheery demeanor. "I feel like I'll never be warm again, but it isn't so much from the weather. It's because of all this."

She swept her arm in a gesture that took in the smashed window, the splintered furniture, and the formerly cheerful dining area, now dominated by a vintage red Ford Mustang.

The car sat diagonally in a sea of glass shards, straddling what had once been a window sign advertising the Wednesday-night special, meatball sandwiches with Cowboy Surprise.

Paul reached out to squeeze LuAnne's shoulder. "I'm so sorry this happened," he told her.

LuAnne folded her arms across her ample

middle. "I know what you mean. I keep havin' to convince myself I'm not in the middle of some awful nightmare."

"How's Loretta?" Paul asked, nodding toward the wiry older woman hunched in the booth with her head cradled in her hands.

LuAnne glanced over her shoulder before answering. "I'm not sure. I think the poor thing's in shock. I mean, can you imagine lockin' up your restaurant just like always, and a few hours later, getting a call that someone used it for a parkin' space?"

"It must have been a terrible jolt," Kate agreed.

"More than a jolt." LuAnne gave her head an emphatic shake that sent wisps of flaming red hair into a wild dance around her temples. "She's spent a bigger part of her life right here in this diner than anywhere else. Why, Loretta practically lives here. Ever since she opened the place forty years ago, it's been more like a home to her than a business."

LuAnne swiped the back of her hand across her eyes. "And I feel the same way. I've been workin' for Loretta since I got out of high school, and we've gotten real close. She's more like family to me than some of my own kin."

She glanced at the gray-haired woman in the booth once more, then pursed her lips and swallowed. "I'm worried about her, to tell you the truth."

Paul turned to Kate. "Why don't I go talk to Loretta while you get your wallet?"

"That's a good idea. Where did you put it, LuAnne?"

"You're going to have to talk to the sheriff about that, darlin'. He has it over there." LuAnne gestured toward the Mustang, then turned and followed Paul to Loretta's booth.

Kate eyed the mangled car, looking for the best way to approach it. Obviously the cleanup crew hadn't been allowed anywhere near the vehicle yet.

She picked her way across the splinters of glass in the clearest section. LuAnne was right, she noted when she drew nearer. The license plate was missing.

And her wallet had been found on the passenger seat.

That fact only added to the dreamlike quality of this mystifying night.

What on earth was going on?

Chapter Two

Sheriff Alan Roberts glanced up from dusting the steering wheel for prints and waved Kate to a stop when she was five feet away.

"I can't let you come any closer, Kate. This is a crime scene." His face looked haggard under the diner's fluorescent lights.

Kate halted obediently and stared at the car's crumpled hood. "Do you have any idea who did this?"

"Nothing yet." The sheriff put one hand behind his neck and rolled his head from side to side.

"We don't even know whose vehicle it is at the moment. There's no sign of the driver. Nothing in the car, either. No license, no registration. There's no identification at all . . . except for this."

He reached through the car's open door and retrieved a clear plastic bag containing a brown calfskin wallet.

Relief swept over Kate. She stepped forward to take the wallet, but the sheriff pulled back his arm. "I can't let you have it, Kate. Not now, at least. It's evidence."

"But I need it," Kate sputtered. "All my identification is in there." She heard the sound of crunching glass and turned to see Paul step up beside her.

She gestured toward the sheriff. "He won't give it back to me. He says it's evidence."

Paul nodded. "Could we at least verify what's inside so she'll know if anything's missing? It would help to know if we need to cancel her credit cards in the morning."

Kate clapped her hand to her mouth. "I hadn't even thought about that."

Sheriff Roberts shook his head. "I can't let you go through it until I've checked it for prints. But it would be a good idea to cancel those cards regardless of whether they were removed from the wallet. Whoever took it could have copied down all the numbers. That's all he would need to be able to charge something to your account online."

A wave of exhaustion washed through Kate. She leaned against Paul for support, and he pulled her snug against his side.

"Ready to go home?" he asked. "I think

you've had enough excitement for one night."

"Not yet." Kate forced herself to stand upright and looked at the chaos around them. "As long as we're here, we ought to pitch in and help."

"I agree, but are you sure you're up to it?"

At her nod, he dropped a kiss on her forehead, then strode over to help Sam and Jack carry a broken tabletop to a pile where fragments of other dining furniture had already been laid to rest.

Kate cast one more look at the mystery vehicle, then glanced around the crowded diner. J. B. Packer, Loretta's part-time cook, stood talking to Lawton Briddle, the mayor of Copper Mill. Kate walked over to them.

"How can I help?"

J.B. smiled at her and pointed to a pair of brooms leaning against the wall. "Grab one of those and start sweeping. We need to move all this trash and debris out of the way so Loretta can get an idea of how bad the actual damage is."

J.B. had been arrested for setting fire to Faith Briar Church when Paul and Kate first arrived in Copper Mill, and although he had been cleared of all charges, he was still regarded with some suspicion in town.

Kate was glad to see him there helping with the cleanup.

The mayor passed the palm of his hand over the few remaining strands of hair on top of his head. "I just can't believe it. Who would do something like this?"

Too tired to carry on a conversation, Kate pondered the question as she maneuvered the broom, pushing broken glass and fragments of wood toward a growing heap at one side of the dining area.

From the talk that swirled around her, she knew the same question was foremost in everyone else's minds as well. Snippets of conversation caught her attention as she worked.

"What kind of person drives into a building and then just up and walks away?"

Kate turned to see who was talking but didn't recognize the wiry man.

"Bunch of joyriders, most likely," answered a heavy-set blonde woman Kate recognized as Elma Swanson. "No responsibility, these kids today. They think nothing of making a mess and leaving it for someone else to clean up."

"You're probably right. Most people would have called it in as soon as the accident happened," J. B. Packer volunteered.

"If it was an accident."

The comment came from Pete Barkley, a man Kate had seen around town from time to time but didn't know well. She pricked up her ears and edged closer to the center of the discussion as she swept.

"What do you mean *if?*" demanded Elma.

Pete leaned on his broom handle and gestured toward the smashed car. "Think about it. Can you really see anyone crashing into the diner like that and then just walking away?" He wagged his head back and forth. "No, sir. Looks to me like it was deliberate."

"That's the craziest idea I ever heard." Elma planted her hands on her broad hips and narrowed her eyes at him. "You mean to tell me you think somebody did this on purpose?"

Kate paused, watching Pete glance around as if realizing the size of his audience for the first time. His chest puffed out slightly when he spoke.

"Wouldn't surprise me a bit. All it would take is someone parking that Mustang across the street on the Town Green and aiming it right at the front door. Then step out of the car, put it in gear, and all you'd have to do is just stand back and let it happen. Boom!" — he smacked his hands together — "There you go."

Several people in the crowd nodded their heads slowly as the idea began to take hold.

Elma just rolled her eyes. "I still say it's crazy. That would mean someone had it in for Loretta or LuAnne, or both. Who on earth would want to do such a thing?"

Who, indeed? Kate wondered as she resumed sweeping. She glanced across the diner at the booth where Loretta Sweet appeared to be rallying. LuAnne sat beside her, patting Loretta's hand. Who could possibly want to harm either one of them?

"Aren't you that preacher's wife?" A voice drew Kate out of her thoughts and back to the moment.

Elma Swanson stood beside her, arms crossed. Kate tried to summon up a smile. "That's right. I'm Kate Hanlon."

"Is it true your purse was found in that car?"

"Just the wallet," Kate replied wearily.

"Your wallet was in that Mustang?" The woman's strident tone drew the attention of the workers nearby.

Kate felt her cheeks grow warm. "That's right."

Elma narrowed her eyes. "Seems like the front seat of a wrecked car is a funny place for a wallet to show up all by itself."

Out of the corner of her eye, Kate saw

Paul approaching with Loretta right behind him, as if drawn by the tension that sizzled through the little group gathered around Kate. He put his arm around her shoulders and pulled her close. "Time to go home."

Kate shook her head. "We can't leave when there's still so much to do."

"Yes, you can." Loretta's tone brooked no argument. "I'm sending everyone home." She stepped up onto the seat of a nearby booth and raised her voice to address the crowd.

"Listen, everybody. I want to thank you all for coming out to help. I've asked Pastor Paul to say a few words." She gestured to Paul, who smiled at the weary faces turned his way.

"Seeing all of you down here tonight is evidence of the fine community spirit that is the heart of Copper Mill, and I know Loretta appreciates your support. While the destruction looks pretty overwhelming at the moment, I'm sure we're all grateful no one was injured. It's not easy to understand why things like this happen, but we can make it through these times of testing with God's help."

"Thank you, Pastor." Loretta commanded the crowd's attention again. "The tow truck just showed up, and some of the men are ready to board up the front as soon as that car is out of here. I'll come back later and see what needs to be done once I can think straight. Until then, I'm going home to try to get some sleep. You all ought to do the same."

Paul leaned forward, his lips next to Kate's ear. "Come on, hon. You've had quite a bit of stress on precious little sleep. You'll feel better once you get some rest."

Too tired to protest, Kate let him lead her toward his pickup. When they reached the sidewalk, she stopped long enough to cast one last look back at the surreal scene.

How could this have happened? And how did she wind up becoming part of it?

Not a single answer came to mind. Kate turned again and followed Paul. She could try to work it out in the morning. All she wanted at that moment was to wipe the sight from her mind and sink back into the comfort of their bed, with Paul beside her.

Chapter Three

"How long will it take to receive my new card?" Kate sighed and jotted a date on the notepad in front of her. "All right. Thank you very much."

She hung up the phone and tapped the end of her pencil on the oak dining table. So much for doing any online shopping in the next few days. It was a good thing she already had plenty of stained-glass supplies on hand. She figured there should be enough to last at least until her new credit cards arrived.

"Rough day?"

Kate jumped at the sound of Paul's voice behind her. He moved closer and started massaging her shoulders with smooth, even strokes.

"I never realized how wearing it could be to cancel a few credit cards. I think I spent half my time on hold and the other half answering calls from church members who wanted to know all the details about the crash."

"What did you tell them?" Paul dug his thumbs into the back of her neck.

Kate closed her eyes and sighed. "What is there to tell? All I know is that my wallet wound up on the front seat of the car that crashed into Loretta's diner, and I have no idea how it got there."

She tipped her head back and grinned up at Paul. "I'm afraid I've let the small-town rumor mill down. I haven't been much help at all."

A chuckle rumbled deep in Paul's chest. "They'll get over it. Did you have any trouble with the credit-card companies?"

"No, everyone was very pleasant once I managed to get past the automated menu and talk to a real live person. It's just that it's going to take a week or more to get the replacements."

She rolled her head gently from side to side, enjoying the way her neck muscles were loosening up under Paul's ministrations.

"The frustrating thing is, I don't even know whether all this is necessary. The cards may still be in my wallet after all."

Paul gave her neck a final rub, then bent over and kissed her on the temple. "Better safe than sorry. Sheriff Roberts was right; it wouldn't take much for someone to write down all the numbers and be able to use them online or over the phone. Has there been any activity on them?"

"Nothing so far." Kate stood and wrapped her arms around Paul's waist. "Maybe canceling them was just an exercise in futility."

"It's still a good thing you called right away. That'll take care of things in case anyone does decide to try to use them."

She laced her fingers behind his neck and leaned into the warmth of his embrace, marveling as she always did at the love she still felt for this man after nearly three decades of marriage. Throughout the years, Paul's ability to make her feel cherished and appreciated had never dimmed.

"Did you stop by for a late lunch? What can I make for you?"

"No, I already ate at JD's Smokeshack. I just stopped by to grab a book I'm going to loan Eli Weston."

Kate stepped back and gave him a mock glare. "Barbecued ribs, right?"

Paul gave her a look of complete innocence. "Excuse me?"

"You've already eaten ribs twice in the last week. You're way over your quota, mister."

Paul threw back his head and laughed. "I won't stray far with you around to keep me in line. Why don't you make something extra healthy tonight to counteract all that nasty cholesterol?"

"It doesn't work that way," she called after him as he headed outside to his truck.

Turning back to the kitchen table, Kate checked off the last of the credit-card companies, relieved to have that chore out of the way. She looked at the rest of her to-do list and wrinkled her nose.

Taking care of those cards had put her way behind schedule, but maybe she could still manage to get a few things done and redeem at least part of the day. She scanned the list to see what would fit into the time available before she needed to fix dinner.

Sun catchers. Kate smiled. Yes, that was it. She would finish the set of butterfly-themed sun catchers she planned to put on consignment at Smith Street Gifts.

Heartened by the idea of doing something productive, she headed for her studio, once their spare bedroom but now her own private creative refuge.

The phone rang when she was just two steps away from the studio door.

Kate glared at the offending instrument. What now? One of the companies she contacted, calling to let her know someone tried to use her card? Or another request for inside information on the crash? Neither possibility sounded appealing.

She wavered, tempted to ignore it, but curiosity drew her back to the kitchen. She could at least check Caller ID.

When she saw the sheriff's office number on the display, she dove for the receiver and snatched it up.

"I just wanted to let you know we're finished with your wallet, Missus Hanlon," Deputy Spencer said. "You can come down to the office and pick it up anytime."

"Thanks so much, Skip." Relief flooded Kate's voice. "I'll be right there."

She started to lower the receiver, then pulled it back to her ear. "By the way, Paul isn't here, and my driver's license is in my wallet. You're not going to cite me for driving without it once I get there, are you?"

The deputy grunted. "That's the least of our worries at the moment. Just drive safe."

Kate grabbed her purse and headed straight to the sheriff's office downtown. The closest parking space she could find was nearly a block away from Town Hall, around the corner on Hamilton Road.

Kate walked up the concrete steps to the brick building that housed the town hall and sheriff's office and pushed through the double glass doors. Turning right, she crossed the creaking wooden floor.

When she opened the door that led into the area used by the sheriff and his deputies, she saw Sheriff Alan Roberts sitting behind a cluttered desk. Though the sheriff's main office was in Pine Ridge, he often worked out of the Copper Mill office. At the front desk, Skip Spencer bent over a stack of paperwork.

Sheriff Roberts scooted his chair back and escorted Kate to a chair in front of his desk before resuming his seat.

"Thank you for finishing up with my wallet so quickly. I can't believe how lost I felt without it."

Kate watched him slide open his desk drawer and pull out her wallet. Clasping her hands in her lap to restrain herself from yanking it out of his grip, she waited for him to pass it to her.

Instead, he set the wallet in front of him and drummed the fingers of his left hand on its calfskin surface. With his right hand, he pulled a legal pad toward him and picked up a pen.

He glanced up at Kate and shrugged. "I'm going to have to ask you a couple of questions while you're here."

Kate shifted in the chair and tried to curb her impatience.

"When did you realize your wallet was missing?"

"When LuAnne called me from the diner."

"When was that?"

"One fifteen this morning," Kate said without hesitation. "I checked the clock when I answered the phone."

He scribbled a few quick notes. "Do you have any idea how you lost it?"

Kate let out a huff of air. "None whatsoever. Paul even wondered if it could have been stolen, but that doesn't seem likely. We don't have much of that kind of thing here in Copper Mill. On the other hand, I can't imagine when I could have lost it." She smiled at him pleasantly. "I guess that puts us back at square one, doesn't it?"

Sheriff Roberts nodded slowly. "How much money did you have in it?"

Kate thought a minute, then shrugged. "About twenty-five dollars, I think. I can't be sure." Her eyes widened. "Is it still there?"

The sheriff handed her the wallet at last. Kate flipped it open and found the bill compartment empty. She stared at him, stricken. "Then someone did steal it?"

He spread his hands wide. "Not necessarily. Someone could have found it and decided they needed the money more than you."

Kate clutched the wallet in both hands. "Well, at least I have my wallet and my identification back. I guess twenty-five dollars is a small price to pay for that. Thanks again for finishing with it so quickly." She tucked the wallet inside her purse and started to rise.

Roberts waved her back to her seat. "Just a minute, Kate. I have a few other things I need to go over with you first. Have you ever seen that Mustang before?"

"Never." Kate shook her head for emphasis. "You mean you still don't know who it belongs to?"

The sheriff stared at his legal pad for a long moment, then fixed his large brown eyes squarely on Kate. "Where were you last night from, say, ten o'clock up until you got the call from LuAnne?"

All the air seemed to rush out of Kate's lungs. "Are you serious?"

An apologetic light shone in the sheriff's eyes, but he let the question hang in the air without answering.

Kate drew herself up and met his gaze without wavering. "I was at home with my husband. You can ask him to verify that, if you feel you need to. Is there anything else?"

"Any idea how the Mustang could have wound up in the middle of Loretta's diner?"

"Sheriff, this is ridiculous! I'm the victim here, not the perpetrator. I never saw that car before in my life. Of course I don't know how it got there."

Kate tried to swallow past the thickness in her throat. She wouldn't give him the satisfaction of seeing her burst into tears. "Am I free to go now?"

"Almost. I just need one more thing from you." He scraped his chair back and gestured her toward the desk where Skip sat, trying not to look like he'd been listening to every word.

"You can be on your way as soon as Skip takes your fingerprints."

Chapter Four

Kate's mouth dropped open. She stared at Sheriff Roberts' impassive face, then looked at Skip, whose dark hazel eyes widened before he dug eagerly into his desk drawer for a fingerprint card and an ink pad.

She looked at the sheriff again. "Please tell me you're joking."

A smile softened his broad face. "Don't get your feathers all ruffled, Kate. It's just routine procedure. Your wallet is the only piece of evidence I have besides that car. I need your prints so I can compare them to the other ones we found at the scene."

He gave her a quick nod, then turned on his heel and left her to Skip.

The deputy inked the pad with gusto, then assumed a solemn expression. "Have you ever been fingerprinted before, Missus Hanlon?"

Kate refused to answer with anything more than a frosty stare.

Skip's cheeks turned bright red. "No, I guess not," he muttered.

He reached for her right hand. Kate stiffened when he pressed her forefinger onto the ink pad.

"Don't try to help, Missus Hanlon. Just let me do it."

I can't believe this is happening. Kate watched, feeling oddly disconnected from the process while he carefully rolled the tip of each finger across its spot on the card, then did the same thing with her left hand.

Now I know how a criminal feels.

Skip handed her a paper towel. "You can use this to clean your hands."

Kate scrubbed at her fingers with the towel and frowned when she saw the dark smudges it left behind. Feeling as vulnerable as she did right now, she wasn't about to go out in public with those telltale marks on her hands.

Digging in her purse, she pulled out a small bottle of hand sanitizer and rubbed the slippery gel over her fingers. She wrinkled her nose at the pungent scent. It didn't remove every last trace of ink, but the result was definitely an improvement.

Without comment, Skip watched her tuck the little bottle back inside her purse, a mildly offended expression his only response.

Leaning across the desk, he spoke in a voice a trifle too loud for the limited office space. "Like the sheriff said, we'll be checking those against the prints we found at the scene . . . especially the ones that were taken from the car."

Did Skip really expect to find a match? She thought he knew her better than that. But his expression, now all business, gave her little clue as to his real feelings.

Choosing not to dignify his statement with a response, Kate turned her back on him. With her head held high, she marched, stiff-legged, toward the exit.

Tears stung her eyes, and she pressed her lips together to keep them from trembling. As bizarre as it seemed, Skip actually appeared to believe she had some part in driving the Mustang through Loretta's diner.

And if local law enforcement already assumed her guilt, what did the rest of the community think?

Kate remembered the barely veiled curiosity on the faces of the cleanup crew at the diner and stifled a groan. From the questions Elma had posed, it was all too evident that some of them already had misgivings about her presence there.

She quickened her pace, suddenly wanting nothing more than to escape Skip's suspicious gaze and fill her lungs with the clear air outside.

Escape? She stopped with her hand on the door. *What am I doing? I'm already acting like I'm guilty! This isn't going to help me a bit.*

Taking a deep breath, she spun around and strode over to Sheriff Roberts. Without asking permission, she resumed her seat in the visitor's chair.

He glanced up, and the crease between his eyebrows deepened. "Is there something I can do for you?"

"As a matter of fact, there is." Kate met his gaze without flinching. "You can tell me what you've learned about the car. Have you been able to find out who it belongs to yet?"

Roberts leaned back in his chair and swiveled it back and forth as though trying to decide how much to tell her. With his mind apparently made up, he straightened and rested his forearms on the desk. "We ran a check on the VIN number this morning."

Kate's spirits rose at the news. "So you know who it belongs to?" Maybe now that they had the name of the owner, this whole miserable episode could soon be put to rest.

The sheriff nodded. "A fellow named Roland Myers." He slanted a look her way. "Do you know him?"

Kate bristled at the implication but kept her tone neutral. "I've never heard of him before. Is he someone local?"

"He has a place way out east of town, off Mountain Laurel Road." He broke off abruptly and stared down at his desk, apparently fascinated by the doodles that decorated the blotter.

He knew more; Kate felt sure of it. She cast about for some way to keep the conversation going. "Had Mr. Myers reported it missing?"

Roberts picked up a pen and twiddled it between his fingers. Kate could almost see the gears turning in his mind.

"No." He finally broke the silence. "And that's the funny thing about it. When we went out to see him this morning, he seemed almost upset to hear we'd found his car."

Chills of excitement skittered up Kate's spine. "Was he the one driving it last night?"

Roberts continued to fiddle with his pen. "According to him, he didn't even know the car was missing until we showed up."

"Did you fingerprint him too?" The words came out before Kate could stop herself.

A slow smile stretched the sheriff's cheeks. "As a matter of fact, we did. There were some old prints that matched his inside the Mustang, but they didn't match the more recent prints we found on the steering wheel and the door."

Kate's hope for a quick resolution to her dilemma faded like the mountain mist on a sunny morning. She sagged against the back of the metal chair. "So it isn't going to be a simple open-and-shut case? You really don't know any more than that?"

"Nope." Sheriff Roberts tossed the pen back onto the desk. "Like you said, we're back to square one."

Kate racked her brains for more questions, but she couldn't come up with any at the moment. She gathered up her purse and stood. "Well, thank you for your time."

She walked to the door, trying to ignore the appraising glance Skip Spencer gave her.

On the way back to her Honda, she slowed when she caught sight of a newspaper vending machine. The latest edition of the *Copper Mill Chronicle* came out on Thursday mornings, so these copies were practically hot off the press. Maybe this issue would have some news on the incident at the diner.

Kate opened her wallet for some change, then realized the coins, as well as the cash, were gone.

Muttering under her breath, she dug around in her coat pockets and came up with enough quarters to drop in the machine slot. When she unfolded the paper, she realized there wasn't just "some" news on the crash — it was "the" news.

A bold headline screamed, DINER DEMOLISHED; DRIVER DISAPPEARS. Below it, the story was splashed across the front page.

Tucking her purse securely under her arm, Kate read as she walked. Jennifer McCarthy, recent college graduate and the *Chronicle*'s reporter, started off with the basic "Who, What, When, Where, Why, and How" formula instilled by the journalism department at the University of Tennessee. Kate skimmed the article, looking for any nuggets of information that might lie within, and was surprised to read about the car's owner.

Acting on a report received at 12:30 a.m. Thursday, officers from the Harrington County Sheriff's Department arrived at the Country Diner to find a 1968 red Ford Mustang sitting in the main eating area.

The car, owned by longtime Copper Mill resident Roland Myers, had apparently been moved from Myers' property sometime late Wednesday evening.

So that was why Sheriff Roberts had been willing to share that tidbit of news with her. He must have given the information to Jennifer McCarthy and known it would soon be public knowledge. He hadn't granted her any special favors after all. Kate sniffed and resumed her reading.

> The identity of the car's driver remains unknown. Despite the substantial damage done to the Mustang and the diner, the person responsible apparently was able to leave the scene of the accident without a trace. At the time this paper went to press, Myers had not responded to requests for comment.

From there the article continued in Jennifer's rather florid style, with quotes from both Loretta and LuAnne about the shock of discovering their place of business smashed to smithereens. J.B. was cited as a great help in cleaning up the mess, though he was only a part-time employee. Kate was ready to refold the paper when a sentence near the end of the article caught her eye:

> Adding yet another twist to this bizarre affair was the discovery of a wallet on the

Mustang's front seat.

Oh no. The paper crinkled under Kate's fingers as she read the rest of the paragraph.

According to the sheriff's office, the wallet belonged to Kate Hanlon, wife of Paul Hanlon, pastor of Faith Briar Church. No definite reason for the wallet's presence inside the stolen vehicle had been discovered by press time, but the sheriff is continuing to investigate.

"Oh, that's just great. More grist for the rumor mill." Kate bunched the paper into a wad and stuffed it under her arm, wondering when Jennifer would get around to questioning her. Maybe she'd already tried to call, but only met with a busy signal. Kate chalked up one positive result of spending so much time on the phone earlier.

But if she thought this morning's spate of phone calls was bad, it would be nothing compared to what would come after this. She could almost hear the tongues wagging now.

Father, please help me. I'm going to need your grace to deal with this.

The downtown area was filled with people going about their business, and it suddenly seemed fraught with peril. Any one of them might stop her and try to strike up a conversation about last night's accident.

Kate had no desire to be accosted or to discuss the situation with anyone until she had time to think and talk it over with Paul.

Ducking her head, she hurried back toward her parking spot. What a nightmare! Her steps clicked along in a quick cadence as she hurried north along Euclid. Only half a block to go.

She rounded the corner at Hamilton and slammed against a solid object in the middle of the sidewalk. Kate cried out and fought to keep her balance, while her purse and newspaper went flying.

What had she hit — a lamppost? Kate's vision cleared, and her breath stuck in her throat. No, she had plowed straight into a man.

Make that a boy, she amended when she got a better look at the skinny teenager in a loose-fitting, brown bomber jacket, who now slumped against the brick storefront only a few feet away.

Kate rushed over to him. "I'm so sorry! It was all my fault. I wasn't watching where I was going." She reached out to help him, but the boy flinched and backed away.

She drew back, remembering how easily

feminine outbursts had embarrassed her son, Andrew, when he was young. "I truly am sorry. Are you hurt?"

The boy stared at the ground and shook his head.

Kate bent to retrieve her purse, but the youth beat her to it, scooping up both the purse and the newspaper and shoving them into Kate's arms.

"Thank you," Kate said. "Are you sure you're all right?"

"I'm fine," the boy mumbled. "Don't worry about it." He hurried away before she could get another word out.

Kate stared after him, confused by his abrupt departure. *Why would he take off like that? He doesn't even know me.*

A wry thought popped into her head. Maybe he had read the article and recognized her as the only known link to the stolen Mustang. Maybe she was just being paranoid, but the possibility was frightening nonetheless.

CHAPTER FIVE

Kate walked into the lobby of the Copper Mill High School gym, more than ready to lose herself in the excitement of rooting for Paul and the Copper Mill church league basketball game. Each church in town had a team, and they played against one another on Friday evenings all winter.

She stepped to one side and leaned against the wall, closing her eyes, listening to the familiar pregame sounds emanating from inside the gym.

A slow smile curved her lips. Yes, this was exactly what she needed to help unravel her tension.

Before she went into the gym, she purchased a Styrofoam cup of hot chocolate at the concession stand, manned by teens from the Copper Mill Presbyterian youth group. The girl behind the counter counted back change and gave Kate a grin that showed off a set of gleaming braces that must have set her parents back a pretty penny.

"Hi, Mrs. Hanlon. Do you remember me?"

Kate frowned, then her brow relaxed. "Of course. You came to a Sunday-morning service at Faith Briar with Brenna Phillips. Carly, right?"

"Close. It's Marlee." The teen flashed another glittering smile. "I guess you've had a lot of excitement lately, huh?"

A ripple of anxiety spread through Kate at the reminder of how far the news had spread. She forced a smile. "More than I ever wanted or expected."

And Lord, please let that be the end of it. She held the cup between her hands and let the fragrant steam tickle her nostrils. "Things should be settling down now, and I'm glad of it."

"That's nice. Hope you enjoy the game."

Kate started to move away, then she spotted a small package of shelled sunflower seeds nestled among the rows of candy bars and chips. Unexpectedly her mouth watered. She hadn't sat around munching sunflower seeds in ages!

It would be the perfect accompaniment to an evening of cheering for the team. She handed Marlee another handful of change, tucked her purse under her arm, and scooped up the cellophane packet.

Inside the gym, the noise grew louder. Kate scanned the crowd, noting a sizable contingent of fans from Faith Briar Church and Copper Mill Presbyterian, out in force to support their teams.

She stood off to one side and took a moment to observe and enjoy the scene. The move she and Paul had made from their fast-paced life in San Antonio to the simpler pleasures of Copper Mill had meant making a number of adjustments, some easier than others. One of the more pleasant surprises had been discovering the way the entire community tended to turn out in support of local events.

And it appeared that night would be no exception. Based on a quick estimate, she guessed that more than a hundred fans had arrived already, and a steady stream continued to pour in through the wide doors.

Kate tore open the cellophane wrapper she was holding and popped a few sunflower seeds into her mouth, enjoying the nutty flavor. Those distinctive warm-up sounds always took her back to her high-school and college days: the squeak of athletic shoes on the shiny hardwood floor, the *whack* of balls against the backboard as players from each team practiced their shots, and a multitude of conversations going on all at once, punctuated by sharp bursts of laughter.

Some things never changed, she reflected. Thank goodness for that.

She moved through the crowd to an open spot at one end of the bleachers on the Faith Briar side and took a tentative sip of her hot chocolate.

Yikes! No complaints about lukewarm beverages here. The steaming brew nearly scalded her tongue. She turned to the sunflower seeds instead, munching them absently while enjoying the sights and sounds of small-town camaraderie.

She watched the constant swirl of activity, the two teams in motion on the floor, people clambering up and down the bleachers. A lone figure standing motionless against the far wall caught her attention. With a start, Kate recognized the victim of her haste the previous day.

The skinny boy stood alone, hands shoved into the pockets of his worn leather jacket. Kate saw a group of teens walk past, glance his way, then keep on walking. The boy looked after them with a lonely expression that tore at Kate's heart.

He was people watching too. His head swiveled from side to side as he looked around the gym, first on the Copper Mill

Presbyterian side, then toward the Faith Briar stands.

When his gaze swept the bleachers near where she stood, Kate smiled and tried to catch his attention, wanting him to know there was at least one friendly face in the crowd.

Maybe she should go over and talk to him for a minute, perhaps apologize again and make sure he didn't have any lasting effects after being slammed into a brick wall because of her carelessness.

But before she could put her plan in motion, the boy stepped through the outer door and slipped out of the gym. As Kate tried to decide whether to follow him, someone bumped against her from behind. She gasped and clamped her arm tighter around her purse, wedging it firmly against her body. After what she'd gone through to get her wallet back, she wasn't about to take a chance on losing it again.

"Kate! Over here!" Livvy Jenner's bright voice rang out over the crowd noises.

Kate spotted Livvy halfway up the bleachers and waved back. She popped the last handful of sunflower seeds into her mouth and tossed the packet into a nearby trash receptacle, then she made her way up the steps to join her best friend.

Livvy, the town librarian, had a methodical mind and a knack for digging up information that had helped Kate unravel mysteries on numerous occasions. Kate counted Livvy's help as a blessing, but valued her friendship even more. Being able to talk to her now was exactly what Kate needed.

"Are you okay?" Kate blurted out when she got close enough to see her friend's puffy eyes and pink nose.

"It's just a cold." Livvy waved away her concern. "I've already started taking vitamin C and zinc tablets. That ought to take care of it. I wasn't about to miss watching Danny and my boys play. How are you doing? I've been worried about you ever since I read that article in the *Chronicle,* but every time I've tried to call, your line has been busy. Has it been awful?"

"I won't say it's been fun, but I'll survive." Kate settled onto the seat next to Livvy. She set her drink on the empty seat in front of her, shrugged out of her coat, and let it settle loosely around her shoulders.

An unexpected yawn stretched her mouth wide, and she clapped her hands over her lips.

Livvy grinned. "Running a little short on sleep, I take it?"

"Maybe I should have gotten coffee instead," Kate joked, retrieving her cup of hot chocolate and cradling it between her hands. "I haven't caught up on my rest since LuAnne called two nights ago."

Livvy's expression grew solemn. "What an awful thing to happen! And I couldn't believe it when I heard about your wallet."

"That makes two of us." Kate sighed. "Although half the town seems more than ready to believe I was the one driving the car."

Livvy's mouth dropped open. "You're joking."

"I wish I were. Once that article came out, the phone hasn't stopped ringing. I spent most of the morning trying to convince the people who called that I didn't have any part in the whole escapade." Kate took a long sip of her hot chocolate. "The calls have started tapering off, so I'm hoping that means things are getting back to normal again."

She scanned the crowd, waving to people she recognized. "Is it just my imagination, or are people staring at me?" she whispered to Livvy.

Livvy giggled. "If you ask me, you're beginning to sound a little paranoid. People may be looking for inside information on the crash, but that hardly makes you the town pariah."

The buzzer sounded, signaling the start of the game. Kate and Livvy turned their attention to the court, where players were taking their places in the midcourt circle, awaiting the tip-off.

The referee tossed the ball into the air. Justin Jenner, Faith Briar's center, slapped it to a waiting teammate, and the game was on.

Kate propped her feet on the empty spot in front of her and leaned forward with her elbows on her knees, ready to follow the action.

Livvy's husband, Danny, pounded down the length of the court ahead of his opponents and flipped in a perfect layup.

"All right! First blood!" Jack Wilson shouted from high in the Faith Briar bleachers.

"Attaboy, Danny," Livvy hollered. "Now get back on defense!"

Kate added her voice to the cheers and eagerly awaited the next play.

"Crazy thing that happened down at the diner the other night, wasn't it?" The male voice behind her sounded a bit like Jim Hepburn, the Humane Society's volunteer dog catcher. He was subdued but still loud enough for her to hear over the noise on the court.

Kate's shoulders tensed, and Livvy gave her a quizzical glance. Without giving any indication that she had heard the comment, Kate tipped her cup to drain the last drops of the sweet chocolate drink.

"No kidding!" The response was a bit louder, but this time Kate couldn't put a name with the voice. "Have they got any idea who did it?"

"Nah, that's a mystery." The first speaker lowered his voice, and Kate strained to hear, all the while reminding herself about the evils of eavesdropping.

"I thought it might have been ol' J. B. Packer, and the sheriff thought so too, but apparently several people saw him out at the Dew Drop Inn, and that cleared him of all suspicion. So no one knows. The even bigger mystery is how Kate Hanlon's wallet got in that car. Did you hear about that?"

His companion snorted. "Yeah, wild isn't it? I mean, her being the pastor's wife and all. I bet there's more to that than she'd like anybody to know."

Kate elbowed Livvy and hissed out of the corner of her mouth. "Paranoid, huh?"

Livvy's eyebrows drew together, but she didn't give an audible response.

Kate wondered whether to turn around and acknowledge the statement or just huddle within the shelter of her coat. She settled for scrunching down in her seat, pulling her coat collar up around her ears.

Like a turtle retreating into its shell, she thought in disgust. Throwing her distaste for eavesdropping to the wind, she edged farther back and tuned in to the rest of the conversation.

"Any word coming out of the sheriff's office about what they've found out?"

The bleachers jiggled slightly, and Kate heard Ronda, one of the stylists at Betty's Beauty Parlor, join the furtive conversation, talking at a mile-a-minute pace.

"Did I hear you two talking about the Mustang that tore up Loretta's place? It's sure a shame the diner's shut down. When is she going to open it back up again?"

Ronda barely paused for breath before going on. "And what was the thing about . . . oh!"

Kate didn't have to turn around to know that her presence had been pointed out. She clenched her hands and felt the foam cup crumple in her fist.

Chapter Six

The crowd erupted into cheers. Kate looked up again. Someone must have scored a basket, but she couldn't have told which team it was. She checked the scoreboard: Faith Briar, 8; Copper Mill Presbyterian, 6.

When did all that happen? She took a deep cleansing breath and made a deliberate effort to regain her focus on the game.

Instead, she noticed for the first time the number of faces that turned her way, then quickly averted their eyes when they saw her looking back.

She leaned to her left and murmured in Livvy's ear. "Are you sure you want to be seen sitting with me? I seem to be drawing as much attention as the game is."

Livvy tore her gaze from the court, where Morgan Carlyle had just blocked Paul's shot.

"What are you talking about? Just because a few people decide to gossip —"

Kate shook her head. "It isn't just that. Take a look around the bleachers. People are staring, and it isn't at the action on the floor."

"I think your imagination is working overtime." Livvy shot a quick glance around the rows of seats below them. Suddenly Kate saw her stiffen, and the rest of her protest died on her lips.

Livvy drew in a breath. "I see what you mean. I'm sorry I didn't take it seriously." Her face tightened, and she reached over to squeeze Kate's hand. "Do you want to leave? I'll go with you, and we can find someplace quiet to talk things over."

"No." Uttering the brief word took a surprising amount of effort. "That would only stir up more speculation."

Livvy looked doubtful. "If you're sure."

Kate squared her shoulders and assumed an air of confidence she didn't feel. "I haven't done anything wrong, and I'm not going to slink away like I'm guilty."

"That's probably the best way to deal with it," Livvy agreed. "It's sure to blow over soon." She patted Kate's hand, then turned her attention back to the game.

Kate ordered herself to ignore the whispers and furtive glances but found that was easier said than done. She remembered her childhood fascination with looking through a pair of binoculars from the wrong end, and the way it made objects close-up appear to be at a great distance.

The same thing seemed to be happening now, without the need for a pair of inverted lenses. Though seated in the midst of a cheering throng, she had the odd sensation of being set totally apart from it all, of looking at familiar things from the far side of a gap she couldn't hope to bridge.

Unbidden, thoughts of all the things she and Paul had done since coming to Copper Mill paraded through her mind. How many times had they reached out to help people in the community? How many times had they encouraged and believed in people everyone else had given up on? Her throat thickened, and she tried to swallow the obstinate lump away. Instead, her throat tightened, and tears threatened to spill over. Kate reached up to dash the moisture from her eyes, hoping Livvy wouldn't notice.

She should have known better. No sooner had she wiped her cheeks with her fingers than Livvy fixed her with a compassionate look that threatened to start her eyes brimming over once more.

Livvy seized Kate's wrist and tugged her to her feet. "Come on," she ordered. "I know you don't want to slink away, but you do need a break from all these prying eyes." She led the way down the bleachers and out to the short hallway that led to the restrooms.

Kate leaned against the wall and attempted a smile. "Just for the record, I feel utterly ridiculous. I didn't mean to make a scene. It's just that . . ."

Tears stung her eyes again, and Kate blinked rapidly to keep them at bay. "It's just that we've worked so hard at fitting in here. Living in Copper Mill is so different from what we knew in San Antonio, but we've tried our best to adapt."

"And you've done an admirable job of it." Livvy spoke with the conviction of a true-blue friend. "I know it hasn't been easy for you."

"No," Kate admitted, "it hasn't. But we truly believe this is where God wants us to be." She drew a long, shaky breath. "Now that we finally feel like we're fitting in, I can't help but wonder if this episode with the runaway Mustang will be the undoing of all our efforts?"

Livvy's eyes widened, and she planted her hands on her hips. "Don't you let yourself think that for a moment, Kate Hanlon! God isn't about to let that happen. Do you really believe he's going to let some crazy incident interfere with his plans? You had nothing to do with what happened at the diner."

"Whether I did or not isn't the point. The point is whether everyone *believes* I did. Once a notion gets planted in people's heads — whether true or not — it's as hard to uproot as . . . as kudzu."

Livvy clicked her tongue. "But all anyone has to do is look at what you and Paul have done since you came here. Look at all the ways you helped rebuild the church. And you were responsible for buying the property next door to set up the food pantry. You're both available to anyone who has a problem, regardless of whether they're a member of Faith Briar. If you weigh all that against one isolated event, any fair-minded person can see which is a true picture of your character."

"But life isn't always fair." A sigh escaped Kate's lips. "Think about it, Livvy. If we've overheard two snippets of gossip just sitting in the stands at a church league basketball game, how much more is being said out around the community?"

Kate's shoulders slumped. "And all because my wallet wound up in a place it shouldn't have been."

Livvy wagged her head back and forth. "I

still think you're making mountains out of molehills. You and Paul are doing your best to do God's work and God's will in this place, right?"

Kate looked down at her tightly knotted hands, then back up at Livvy. "Right, but no matter how hard we try, that doesn't mean things will always go the way we want them to."

Livvy's hazel eyes shone with compassion, and she reached out to grip Kate's shoulders. "No, but it does mean this is *God's* work, not yours. Quit beating yourself up for things you can't change, and let him take care of it. He knows what he's doing."

This time the tears that sprang to Kate's eyes were tears of joy. She gave Livvy a quick hug. "Thanks for the reminder. You're such a wonderful friend."

She followed Livvy back to their seats with a far lighter heart. God was in control; all she had to do was follow his lead. How had she lost sight of that simple truth? He had brought them to Copper Mill. She knew that beyond the shadow of a doubt. His plans and his timing were perfect.

A sudden thought dimmed her optimism. What if she and Paul had been placed in Copper Mill for a season and were meant to move on from there to start over again somewhere else?

Her throat tightened again at the idea. As different as Copper Mill was from anything she had known before, the thought of leaving hurt more than she ever would have dreamed.

But what if that proved to be the case? Maybe their stay in Copper Mill had only been a time of testing. And what a test she was going through right now!

How am I supposed to handle this, Lord? Never before had she faced dealing with people who questioned her integrity or wondered what kind of shenanigans she had been up to.

"Way to go, Pastor Paul!"

Kate jerked her head up in time to see the ball swish into Faith Briar's basket. Paul had just made a three-point shot.

The halftime buzzer sounded, and the jubilant Faith Briar team gathered around Paul, pounding him on the back. Wearing a victorious grin, he looked up, his eyes searching for Kate in the bleachers.

She fixed a bright smile on her face and clapped enthusiastically, determined to hide her bleak thoughts. The idea that something she hadn't done, but was being blamed for, had the potential to hurt the man she loved wrenched at her heart.

It had been a big decision for Paul to make the move to Copper Mill, but once the choice had been made, he'd thrown himself, heart and soul, into his new position. What would the cloud of suspicion brought on by all the gossip do to him?

Maybe he would never have to deal with it. Not if she could solve the mystery before the whispers reached him.

Around her, people got to their feet and headed for the gym floor. Livvy stood and grinned at Kate.

"How about some popcorn? All that talking has made me hungry."

Kate started to rise, then decided against it. If she stayed put, she wouldn't be forced to mingle or talk to anyone.

"I'm fine," she said. "But you go ahead."

Livvy nodded and hurried to join the throng heading toward the concession stand.

Kate pulled her coat up over her shoulders again and looked around the gym. Everyone else in the building, it seemed, was talking, joking, enjoying the evening and the companionship of friends.

Down at the Faith Briar bench, Paul was laughing at something with the rest of the team. Only Kate sat in solitude, an island of loneliness in a sea of conviviality.

She hadn't felt so isolated since they left San Antonio.

By the time the buzzer signaled the second half of the game, Kate had determined to pull herself out of her doldrums by choosing a brighter attitude. She would ignore what was going on around her and pay more attention to the rest of the game. It was the least she could do for Paul. For Livvy.

For herself.

To her relief, the ploy worked, boosting her spirits enough so that she was able to concentrate on the action on the court and join Livvy in shouting encouragement to Faith Briar's team. Thankfully, the rest of the crowd appeared just as caught up in the intense action, focusing more on the game than on speculation about her wayward wallet.

Kate watched the score seesaw back and forth, shaking off her blues enough to cheer wildly when Paul scored two more baskets.

The clock on the scoreboard clicked off the remaining minutes in the game, with Faith Briar hanging on to a scant lead.

Then Copper Mill Presbyterian made a desperate last-ditch rally, increasing their score until only two points separated the teams.

The players raced up and down the court, the tension growing by the second until, with a mighty effort, Paul blocked a three-point shot that would have won the game for the Presbyterians.

The crowd roared and rose to its feet as the final buzzer sounded.

Down on the court, members of the opposing teams shook hands, with a few good-natured jibes thrown in from both sides. As the players filed away to the locker rooms, the Copper Mill Presbyterian coach struck a pose and grinned.

"We'll be back," he yelled, doing a bad Schwarzenegger imitation. His jibe got the desired response, as laughter rose around the gym.

Kate took her time slipping her arms into her coat and gave the bleachers a chance to clear out. Livvy lingered beside her, as if sensing Kate's desire to keep her distance from the rest of the spectators. Together they descended the bleachers and waited while the crowd filtered out of the gym.

Danny and Justin emerged from the locker room. Livvy waved but didn't move to join them.

Kate chuckled and nudged Livvy with her elbow. "You don't have to hover over me, you know. I'll be fine . . . really. Go on and celebrate with your family."

Livvy's eyes sparkled. "I'm glad you're feeling better. Have a great evening, and we'll talk soon."

A short time later, Paul appeared from the locker room, carrying his sports bag in one hand. Feeling carefree for the first time since she entered the gym, Kate hurried over to him and planted a kiss on his cheek. "Congratulations. That was quite a game."

"Wasn't it great?" Paul pumped his fist into the air. "If I hadn't been able to block that shot, it might have gone the other way."

"You're right! They couldn't have done it without you." Kate slipped her arm around his waist and snuggled against his side, feeling as though she had finally reached safe harbor after the storm of suspicion.

Paul pushed open the outer door with his free hand, and their feet crunched across the gravel parking lot. He tossed his sports bag onto the seat of his pickup.

"Some of the guys are going to JD's Smokeshack to celebrate. Are you in the mood for barbecue?" He waggled his eyebrows. "I'll even let you ride along with me, and we can pick up your car on the way back home."

Even by the dim glow of the parking lot lights, Kate could see the excitement in his clear blue eyes. He looked like a little boy offering to share his favorite toy. But she didn't think she could endure being the target of more stares and whispers this evening.

"The Smokeshack is going to be awfully crowded on Friday night," she hedged. She didn't want to dampen his joy by telling him about the speculation swirling through the community or the dark thoughts clouding her mind.

She fixed a bright smile on her lips. "And barbecue sounds a little heavy this late, anyway. What do you say to going home and letting me whip up a frittata for you? We can talk about the game, and you can give me all the details from the player's point of view."

She held her breath, wondering if he would see through her subterfuge.

"An evening talking basketball with my favorite girl?" Paul dropped her a wink that sent a pleasant shiver down her spine. "That sounds like a plan."

He reached for the driver's door of her Accord, parked next to his pickup, and helped her inside. Leaning over, he tapped his forefinger on the tip of her nose. "I'll see you at home."

Relief swept through Kate, and she

grinned back at him. "I'll be right behind you."

She waited for him to start his pickup and followed as he turned left onto Smoky Mountain Road, breathing a prayer of thanks for his willingness to leave the celebration to the others. An evening at home together would be just the thing to dispel her gloom.

Chapter Seven

Trust in the LORD with all your heart and lean not on your own understanding; in all your ways acknowledge him, and he will make your paths straight.

Kate stared at the familiar words in Proverbs and traced them lightly with her forefinger. She had committed those verses to memory many years ago, but that particular morning they seemed to take on a deeper meaning in light of her current situation.

She took a long sip of fresh-ground coffee, then rested her elbows on the arms of her rocker. She leaned her head back against the chair and closed her eyes.

Lord, I really do need to lean on you. I hate not knowing what's going on here. Please help me find out the truth. Give me guidance and make my paths straight.

He would do just that; she felt sure of it. Kate closed her Bible with a renewed feeling of direction, a sense of purpose she hadn't felt since LuAnne's call interrupted her sleep three nights earlier.

She padded to the kitchen, rinsed her coffee mug, and set it on the countertop, optimism welling up within her. God would direct her steps, and it would all work out in the end.

She would follow her instincts, poke around a bit, and see what she could find out. Maybe she wouldn't be able to track down the identity of the Mustang's mystery driver, but with God's help, she would at least see her name cleared.

But where to start? She had solved a number of puzzles for others since coming to Copper Mill, so a bit of sleuthing was nothing new to her. But this time she would be doing it on her own behalf.

Kate pulled out the notepad she used two days earlier when calling the credit-card companies. Carrying it to the kitchen table, she tore off the top sheet and started a new list.

When she completed her list, Kate read through the items and tapped the end of her pencil against her bottom lip. Surely she could come up with something better than that!

"Make my path straight, Lord," she whispered.

She doodled on another sheet of paper while her mind went back over what she knew of the case so far.

Point one: sometime in the wee hours on Thursday morning, Roland Myers' Mustang was driven into the Country Diner.

Flipping to a new page, Kate tore off a fresh sheet of paper and made a quick sketch of a car hurtling through the diner's front window.

Point two: nobody knows who was behind the wheel, as the driver disappeared before the sheriff arrived.

She thought a moment, then added a set of footprints heading away from the scene.

Point three: someone reported the crash to the sheriff's department. Then Loretta and LuAnne were notified and summoned a crew of workers to help with the cleanup.

Kate drew a cluster of cartoonlike circles representing the faces she and Paul had seen when they arrived at the diner.

Point four: my wallet was discovered on the Mustang's passenger seat, and no one has any idea how it got there.

She penciled a small rectangle next to the car, with a series of question marks above it.

Point five: people suspect me of having some involvement with the incident.

Without conscious thought, she added down-turned mouths to the cluster of faces.

Point six: Roland Myers never reported the theft of the car and seemed upset when he learned it had been found.

A rough sketch of Myers' house went in the upper corner of the paper. With a few quick strokes, Kate added a mysterious shadow hanging over the house.

Point seven . . .

There is no point seven, Kate thought gloomily, unless she counted the flurry of talk buzzing around town.

She studied her sketch, hoping for inspiration to strike, but inspiration appeared to be on vacation. No matter how she looked at the situation, it always came down to the same few elements: the car, the diner, the people. Nothing there sparked any new ideas.

Unless . . .

Was there something about the diner? A wisp of memory returned, the conversation between Pete Barkley and Elma Swanson about someone having it in for either LuAnne or Loretta or both.

Did Loretta or LuAnne have a secret enemy? Kate dismissed the idea. On the other hand, stranger things had happened. She knew some people didn't like or trust

J. B. Packer, but he only worked part-time at the diner. Crashing into the SuperMart in Pine Ridge, where he stocked shelves, would have been a better way to get to him.

What about the crowd of recruits who showed up at the diner to help clean up the rubble? Kate remembered the old adage about criminals returning to the scene of the crime.

Could the same thing have happened in this case? It would have been a simple enough matter for the unknown driver to abandon the Mustang and wait in a pocket of darkness, ready to blend in with the band of volunteers when they arrived.

Kate's pulse quickened. Had she been face-to-face with the mystery driver?

She closed her eyes, trying to envision the late-night scene. If only she could remember the faces, she might be able to resolve this dilemma in short order.

She could picture LuAnne and Loretta. Sheriff Roberts, of course, and Skip Spencer. Pete Barkley and Elma Swanson. J. B. Packer standing next to Mayor Briddle. She knew J.B. well enough to know that he would have admitted to it if he had crashed the car. Besides, he had already been cleared. Who else?

Kate tried harder to concentrate, but the

faces swam before her in a blur. It was no use. She had been too tired, too distraught over the discovery of the loss of her wallet to pay close attention to what was going on around her.

She added "Ask LuAnne and Loretta who was there" to her list. Maybe that would be the place to start, since she couldn't find out anything more about the car on her own.

Or could she?

Sheriff Roberts had handed her one important piece of information: the name of the Mustang's owner. And according to him, Roland Myers lived "way out east of town off Mountain Laurel Road."

Excitement buoyed Kate even more than her morning jolt of caffeine. If nothing more, it was a place to start.

Seizing the pencil, she circled Roland Myers' name with a flourish, then snatched up her car keys and purse and headed for the front door.

Kate scanned the mailboxes that marked the sparsely scattered properties along Mountain Laurel Road. It was a shame Livvy couldn't come with her. She seemed to know where everybody lived. But waiting for Livvy to get off work would have meant a delay of several hours, and everything within Kate demanded action right away.

There it was. Kate turned when she spotted the rusty mailbox with peeling remnants of the name "Myers" stenciled in black paint on its side. Gravel crunched beneath the tires of her Honda Accord as she made her way up the long rutted driveway.

To either side, derelict cars in different stages of dismemberment littered the ground.

Like an automotive graveyard. Kate shuddered when the thought sprang into her mind, then laughed at her flight of fancy.

The house, a white frame building with peeling paint, sat just beyond. Kate parked her Accord beside a decrepit International Scout sitting up on blocks. From the looks of things, the aging vehicle must have been laid to rest there years before. The trunk of a small sapling poked through one of the side windows.

She lifted a plate of brownies from the passenger seat and picked her way through the maze of auto bodies and assorted parts, still fighting down the feeling she was in some sort of bizarre cemetery.

Maybe it wasn't such a surprise the man hadn't reported the theft of the Mustang any sooner. Amid all this clutter, why would he notice one missing vehicle?

The screen door squeaked, and a slight man with sunken cheeks stepped out onto the sagging front porch. He watched Kate in silence, snapping one of his suspender straps against his faded red flannel shirt while she navigated the obstacle course.

Kate tried to size him up and keep her footing at the same time. He seemed harmless enough, with a pleasant expression and graying hair that fringed three sides of his head.

When she reached the porch at last, she held up the brownies and offered him her brightest smile.

"Mr. Myers? I'm Kate Hanlon. My husband is the pastor of Faith Briar Church. We haven't had the chance to meet you yet, so I brought this for you as a sort of get-acquainted gift."

His lips parted in a gap-toothed grin. "You ain't from around here, are you?"

Kate's shoulder muscles tensed, but she kept smiling. "Do you know Faith Briar? It's the little white church near the high school."

Myers chortled. "That may be, but you didn't get that twang from anywhere in these parts."

Kate's shoulders relaxed, and she smiled

in earnest. "I see what you mean. No, I'm not from around here. My husband grew up about an hour away from Copper Mill, but I'm originally from Texas."

"Thought so." The old man's gaze shifted from Kate to the plate of brownies and back again. "My Mildred used to bake once a week. Wednesday — that was always her baking day."

He leaned against the porch rail, and his eyes took on a faraway look. "Nothing like the smell of homemade brownies, fresh from the oven."

He reached out to take the plate from Kate's hands and held it up to his nose. Sniffing appreciatively, he let out a wistful sigh. "It's been a long time since I smelled something that good. Thank you kindly."

He reached for the handle of the screen door and tugged it open a few inches. "Would you like to come in? The place isn't fancy, but I could brew up a pot of coffee that would go good with these brownies. Seems like the least I can do, since you managed to make your way through all that mess."

His comment called Kate back to the reason she had come. She mounted the first porch step and waved her arm in an arc, taking in the accumulation of cars. "You do have quite a collection here, don't you?"

Myers' laugh ended on a wispy wheeze. "You're right as rain about that. Mildred used to call it a regular junkyard."

Taking her cue from that, Kate watched him closely as she added, "Didn't that Mustang belong to you? The one that crashed into the Country Diner?"

The old man's grin disappeared like a flash. He ducked his head in a jerky nod. Kate could see his Adam's apple bounce up and down like the basketball at Friday night's game.

She pressed on. "Such a terrible thing! It must have been a shock to you when you found it missing."

The handle slipped from Myers' fingers, and the screen door slapped against the frame. His face darkened and took on a shuttered expression, and the friendly light left his eyes.

"I've talked to the sheriff, and that's all I'm gonna say about it." He thrust the plate of brownies back into her hands. "You ain't bribin' any answers out of me with a phony gift. You'd best be goin'." He folded his arms across his scrawny chest and stood his ground.

Kate looked at the plate, then balanced it carefully on the porch railing. "I'm sorry if

I offended you, but the gift wasn't phony. Please keep it and enjoy it."

Feeling like an utter hypocrite, she made her way back to her car. *Well, that didn't go well.*

Or maybe she had gained more information than she knew. Something had triggered that sudden change in Roland Myers' demeanor . . . but what?

She hadn't accused him of anything, hadn't voiced any sort of suspicion. But his manner seemed more like a guilt-ridden perpetrator than that of the innocent victim of a car theft.

What was he hiding?

She put the car into gear and cast a last glance around the property. What did one man do with so many broken-down old cars?

Kate caught her breath as she eased her car back toward Mountain Laurel Road. What were those operations called, where stolen cars were cannibalized for their parts?

She thought back to an investigative report on the subject that she had watched in San Antonio. A chop shop! That was it.

She turned onto Mountain Laurel. Could diminutive Roland Myers be running a chop shop on his property? She turned the idea over in her mind and nodded slowly. That could explain his delay in notifying the sheriff about the missing Mustang.

Kate pressed on the accelerator, and her thoughts seemed to pick up speed as well. Reporting the theft would only draw attention to himself and the illicit operation at his property, the last thing Roland Myers would want to do if he were involved in some illegal activity.

Kate pursed her lips and started whistling, then she broke off with a chuckle when she recognized the tune as the theme song from *Cops.*

"Don't celebrate too soon," she told herself. Her theory made sense, but she had no proof other than her instinct. Not yet, anyway.

Chapter Eight

Kate balanced an insulated carrier containing a fresh-from-the-oven casserole dish against her left hip as she opened the front doors of the church, then she slipped across the foyer and tiptoed downstairs with only minutes to spare.

Avery Griffin, the part-time custodian Paul had recently hired, was scooting the last of the folding tables into a straight line. The lines in his round face deepened when he turned a shy smile her way.

"Morning, Mrs. Hanlon. Looks like we have a good turnout today. Good thing there's plenty of food in there."

Kate smiled and nodded, too out of breath to respond aloud. Inside the kitchen, she set the pan of sour-cream chicken enchiladas on a warming tray and took a moment to catch her breath and massage her arthritic knee. It wasn't like her to run late for a Sunday service, but she had taken special pains preparing the casserole that morning.

The whole church would be gathering downstairs after the worship service for the potluck meal, and she wanted to make something especially tasty. Something that would remind the congregation that their pastor's wife was a normal, upstanding person, not the type to be involved in grand theft auto or a hit and run.

And it was just a reminder, she told herself. Not a bribe. Not really.

Lord, help my motives to be pure. To want to do my best to serve others, not just put a positive spin on things for my own sake.

From the looks of the laden table, she wasn't the only one who had put forth an extra effort that morning. During her time in Copper Mill, she had learned that the ladies of the church — and some of the men as well — went all out when it came to these potluck meals.

A fellowship meal always brought out a wide range of dishes and culinary talents. She noticed a hamburger casserole in a plain aluminum pan sitting next to paprika-sprinkled deviled eggs, artistically arranged on a cut-glass platter.

Kate smiled when she recognized the platter. Only Renee Lambert would bring what was likely to be a family heirloom to a church potluck.

Lilting notes from the organ filtered down the stairwell and called her back to the moment. Kate slid the casserole dish from its insulated carrier and trotted upstairs to the sanctuary, where Sam Gorman leaned over the keyboard, letting worship flow from his heart through his fingers in a majestic prelude.

On her way to her seat in the second pew, she spotted Danny Jenner, flanked by his teenage sons, Justin and James. Kate peered past the trio, hoping for a glimpse of Livvy.

Danny smiled at her knowingly and shook his head. "Livvy isn't here, Kate. She's home nursing that cold. The way she's been wheezing and coughing, I told her she'd better take care of herself, or it's going to turn nasty on her."

Kate nodded, feeling bereft. She longed to see Livvy's smiling face, even more to talk to her and get more of her perspective on the diner situation.

She forced a smile, reflecting that she seemed to be doing a lot of that lately. "Tell her I missed her, would you? I'll give her a call this afternoon so we can catch up on things."

"It won't do you any good." Danny's wry smile softened the words. "Her voice is pretty near gone."

"Yeah," James put in with a chuckle. "She can barely make herself squeak."

"Oh. Well, then, tell her to take care of herself, and let her know I'm praying for her."

She settled into her seat, trying to shake off the feeling of being abandoned. It wasn't anything of the sort, she knew. Livvy would be there in a heartbeat to lend moral support and a healthy dollop of common sense if she could.

Kate lifted her chin and tried to look as if this was a Sunday morning just like any other. Deep in her heart, though, she knew it was only an act. She wondered how many in the congregation knew that as well.

Kate sat up straight in the oak pew and smoothed her linen skirt down over her knees. She had dressed with extra care that morning, wanting to present the picture of an eminently respectable pastor's wife.

Paul stepped behind the pulpit and raised his voice enough to be heard over the murmur of voices.

"Let's praise the Lord this morning. Please stand and join me in singing 'How Great Thou Art.' "

Kate stood and walked to the front as the choir assembled on the stage, then let her voice mingle with the others as they all sang one of her favorite hymns. Normally the words flowed freely, but on this occasion she couldn't force them past the lump in her throat.

The same thing had happened the first time she sang that hymn in this building, but then it was due to her gratitude at God's provision in helping the members of Faith Briar rebuild their church from a pile of ashes.

This Sunday she felt more out of place than ever, since the day of their arrival in Copper Mill. *Is this really happening, Lord? It seems more like a bad dream.*

As the final notes of the hymn faded away, Paul gave the congregation the signal to be seated, and she settled back into the pew.

Standing behind the pulpit, Paul looked especially handsome in his favorite navy suit. Every strand of his salt-and-pepper hair was in place. He opened his Bible and gazed out over the assembled worshippers.

"This morning my text comes from Daniel, chapter six."

Paul waited while pages rustled and members of the congregation located the spot in their own Bibles. Then he went on to read the familiar story about Daniel, the man of God, and his steadfastness in the face of adversity. Though lies and gossip threatened his standing and tested his faith, he remained strong.

Kate squirmed. Paul couldn't have chosen a better topic to fit her situation. But how could he have known? She hadn't said a word to him about the talk swirling around town.

Comments she had heard over the years from members of their congregation in San Antonio drifted into her mind: "Have you been reading my mind, Pastor Paul?" "You sure stepped on my toes during that sermon."

Now she knew how they must have felt.

Paul set his Bible on the oak pulpit and looked out over the crowd. "The story is one we've all heard since childhood."

He leaned on the pulpit, and a broad grin split his face. "Have you ever felt like you've been thrown to the lions?"

More than you know. Kate tried to keep her focus on what Paul was saying, but her thoughts kept straying to the people sitting around her. Were they paying attention to the sermon or, like her, were they jittery and distracted by recent events?

With an effort, she pulled her attention back to the front of the sanctuary. Paul looked so happy, so content up there on the platform. The move to Copper Mill had been good for him.

A murmur of assent rippled through the sanctuary, telling her she might not be the only one for whom Paul's question struck home. Kate shifted ever so slightly in her seat so that she could catch a glimpse of the people in the rows behind her.

There was Joe Tucker, a look of rapt attention on his wizened face. One of his gnarled hands rested on the pew in front of him. Kate smiled as she watched his fingers stroke the smooth grain of the wood he had crafted with his own hands.

On the far side of the aisle, she spotted Renee Lambert, resplendent in a pink designer suit, her hair and nails freshly done. Beside her, an oversized Gucci tote in a matching shade of pink rested on the pew. While Kate watched, the bag appeared to move slightly of its own accord, and Renee reached down to pat it with one hand.

Kate tried hard not to smile, knowing Renee's pet Chihuahua, Kisses, was undoubtedly inside the cavernous bag. He accompanied Renee everywhere she went.

His presence during their worship services had taken Kate off guard at first, but the little dog tended to be well behaved. As long as he maintained his usual good manners and didn't decide to accompany the singing or yip during the sermon, she could handle it.

Directly behind Renee, Eli Weston leaned forward with his gaze focused directly at the pulpit, as if determined not to miss a single word of Paul's sermon.

Kate studied these three people she had grown to know and love during their time in Copper Mill. People whose actions and attitudes alternately filled her with affection and exasperation.

What was going through their minds right now? After all the years she and Paul had been in ministry together, she thought she had become used to living in the proverbial goldfish bowl that was an inevitable part of being a pastor's wife.

But here in this smaller setting, it sometimes seemed like the focus had narrowed and magnified, putting them under even more intense scrutiny than they'd been under back in San Antonio.

And what if those observing saw the picture a little out of focus? It only took a slight change of opinion to form a crack in the foundation of trust that could widen into a major rift. Cold fingers of apprehension threaded their way up her spine.

Get ahold of yourself! God has not given

you a spirit of fear. Things couldn't be as bad as she thought they were. Surely she was overreacting, imagining a cloud of suspicion and doubt where there was none.

A rustling in the sanctuary caught her attention, and Kate realized that people were bowing their heads for the closing prayer. While Paul's confident voice gave thanks for God's faithfulness to his people, Kate breathed a heartfelt prayer of her own: *Help me to be faithful, to follow wherever you lead me. And help me to let your people know we love them and are here to serve them.*

After the service, some people stood chatting in small groups, while others, led by LuAnne Matthews, hurried downstairs to the kitchen to finish last-minute preparations for the meal.

Kate looked around, aching for someone to talk to. Eli Weston stopped in the aisle next to her and held out his hand.

"Morning, Kate. How's it going?"

Kate clasped his hand, grateful beyond words to Eli for not mentioning anything about Mustangs, wallets, or demolished diners.

Her lips curved in a rueful smile. "Let's just say it's been an interesting few days."

Eli laughed. "So I've heard. Hang in there. This, too, shall pass." He gave her a warm, encouraging smile before moving on.

Kate scanned the crowd. A cluster of people near the organ were talking in low voices with their heads close together. They looked up as her gaze swept over them. She offered a determined smile and received the same in return. But were those smiles a little chillier than usual?

Lifting her chin, she strode down the center aisle to join Paul near the doors that opened into the foyer. She nodded to the chatting groups as she passed.

This is just like any other Sunday, she reminded herself. But the distance from the front pews to the back of the sanctuary had never seemed so long.

"What was the pastor thinking?" The tart comment came from Millie Lovelace, the church secretary, who averted her eyes when Kate walked past.

Kate's steps faltered, then she kept on moving, deciding to pretend she hadn't heard. *What now?*

She reached Paul at last as he stood talking to Renee Lambert and Joshua "Old Man" Parsons. She was more than ready for him to bestow a welcoming smile on her. Instead, she saw a frown creasing his forehead. None of the three seemed aware of her presence.

Kate's stomach clenched. There would be no danger of overeating at the potluck that afternoon. At this rate, she would be lucky if she could keep even a few bites down.

Old Man Parsons leaned forward, putting his lined face only inches from Paul's. "It was a bad idea, Pastor. You should have checked with some of us first."

Kate stiffened and felt the knot in her stomach grow. Mr. Parsons was one of Faith Briar's longtime members, and in spite of his advanced age of ninety-three, the man was still sharp in mind and tongue.

What on earth was going on?

Paul's face maintained its diplomatic smile, but Kate could tell it took an effort to do so.

"I've already told you how I came to hire him." His calm tone soothed Kate in spite of the tension that emanated from the group. "I saw him slip into the back pew several weeks ago, just after the morning service started. When I came back here to greet him after the service, he asked if he could make an appointment to speak with me —"

"*Speak* to you," Parsons cut in. "Not apply for a job."

Kate sucked in her breath. They were talking about Avery Griffin.

Paul ignored the interruption. "Without breaching confidentiality, I can tell you he didn't come in angling for a job. He's trying to get his life back on track and was looking for someone he could be accountable to. I felt honored that he chose me — and this church — to turn to."

"That still doesn't explain putting him on the payroll." Renee shifted the pink Gucci bag to the other arm and lifted Kisses out of its depths.

"He didn't hint around for a job here, if that's what you're implying," Paul said. "He told me he wanted to find work and was willing to take anything available. I knew we needed someone to clean the church, so I offered the position to him. As I saw it, it was an opportunity to extend grace."

He looked at Old Man Parsons and Renee Lambert in turn. "Don't we all deserve a second chance? Where would any of us be if God never gave us a chance to start over?"

Parsons snorted. "The man's had a second chance. A third and fourth one too. Some people are just too far gone to deserve a helping hand."

Beside him, Renee nodded like a sage. "I'm afraid I have to agree. The man has fallen off the wagon more than once."

Kisses, released from his confinement in

the oversized bag, squirmed in her arms. Renee massaged the spot between his ears with the tip of one French-manicured fingernail before continuing. "You may be putting the church in jeopardy just by having him on the premises."

"That's exactly what I've been saying." Old Man Parsons raised a bony fist and brought it down against the palm of his other hand. "Give the man a key, leave him alone down here when he's supposed to be cleaning, and you know what's bound to happen?"

His bushy white eyebrows bristled as he glared at Paul. "He'll clean the place, all right. Clean it out! Next thing you know, that fancy computer of yours will wind up in some pawn shop in Chattanooga, and you'll never see it again."

Kate glanced around, thankful to find Avery standing by himself in a far corner of the sanctuary, hopefully out of earshot. That was doubtful, though, considering the way Old Man Parsons tended to speak several decibels louder than necessary.

Trying not to look like she was staring, she watched Avery shift from one foot to the other. With his slight build and nondescript coloring, it would be easy for him to blend into the background. That seemed to be the case that morning, as Kate noted several people walk past him without a second glance.

He shot a quick look toward the rear of the sanctuary from time to time, as though he knew their little group was talking about him, and he wanted to pretend he wasn't aware of it.

Kate knew exactly how he felt.

She nudged Paul's elbow and jerked her head slightly in Avery's direction, hoping he would pick up on her signal.

He flicked a quick glance toward her and gave a barely perceptible nod. His smile broadened, and he reached out to grip Old Man Parsons' shoulder.

"From the smells coming from the kitchen, I'd say we have a delectable meal waiting for us. Why don't we set this aside for now? I'll stop by your place tomorrow, and we can talk more about your concerns then."

The old man's eyes narrowed, but he shuffled off toward the stairwell. "Fine, but don't expect me to go home and forget about this. I'll expect you tomorrow."

Just as Kate started to relax, Parsons raised his reedy voice a notch higher and added, "Mark my words, nothing good will come of having a drunk on the premises."

"Oh no!" Kate clapped her hand to her mouth and whirled around. The corner where Avery had been standing was vacant.

She looked up at Paul and caught him by the sleeve. "Avery must have slipped out. Do you think he heard?"

"Are you kidding? The Presbyterians, the Episcopalians, and the Baptists heard that." He kept his tone light, but the grim look on his face told Kate he was every bit as disturbed by the outburst as she was.

He took her by the arm and led her into the foyer. Stopping at the head of the stairs, he gave her a wry grin. "Ready for some fun and fellowship?"

Chapter Nine

"Sorry, lady. I can't help you." The grease-covered mechanic wiped his hands on an even greasier rag and eyed Kate's Honda. "But if you want your tires rotated, we've got a special this week."

"Not today, thanks." Kate climbed back into her car and cast a doleful glance at LuAnne, who waited in the passenger seat. "That's the second auto-repair shop that says they've never done business with Roland Myers. What now?"

LuAnne patted her red hair into place. "We keep on goin', that's what. There's only one more place. Let's check it out."

"Are you sure? I've taken up most of your afternoon as it is."

LuAnne snorted. "Like I have anything but time on my hands these days. With the diner closed down, I'm bored half out of my mind, so you're doin' me a favor by giving me something to do. Besides, I'd like to have a hand in catchin' the scoundrel who put me out of work. Let's get going, darlin'. You never know when a clue is gonna turn up."

She winked at Kate. "And if we strike out at the next place, we'll head over to Emma's Ice Cream and drown our sorrows in a hot-fudge sundae."

Kate summoned up a grin in response, hoping to convey a cheerfulness she was far from feeling. She started the engine and put the car in gear. "You're on."

Following LuAnne's directions, she drove to Bernie's Body Shop at the south edge of Copper Mill. Since Roland Myers lived out east of town, she doubted they would fare any better at this place than the other two. Still, she didn't want to hurt LuAnne's feelings.

And if three strikes were the criteria for deserving that sundae . . .

"Right here," LuAnne announced. "Turn quick, or you'll miss the driveway."

Kate made a quick right turn, followed by an even quicker application of her brakes. The tiny patch of ground that served as Bernie's parking lot was barely big enough to squeeze into.

She surveyed the body shop's scruffy exterior as she and LuAnne exited the

Honda. The building looked as if it had been standing there since the 1930s at least, with its last coat of paint having been applied somewhere back around World War II.

A bluetick hound lay sleeping in a shaft of afternoon sun between the car and the door marked Office. LuAnne strode past with a brisk, no-nonsense step. Kate approached with a bit more caution.

When Kate drew even with the dog, it cracked one eye open long enough to register the presence of two newcomers, flopped the tip of its tail a couple of times, then went back to its nap.

Kate caught up to LuAnne and murmured, "This doesn't look very promising, does it?"

LuAnne refused to be pessimistic. "On the contrary, darlin', this is just the kind of place we're looking for. Bernie's always workin' on some kind of old beater. Just the sort who might be buying used parts. I should have put him at the top of the list right off."

Taking the lead, LuAnne pulled open the grimy glass door and sailed through the tiny office to the work bay on the other side.

The moment they entered the shop, the combined smells of grease and gasoline permeated Kate's nostrils, and she had to make an effort not to sneeze. Most of the bay was taken up by a Chevy pickup with rusted-out side panels — a better candidate for a junkyard than a repair shop, in Kate's opinion.

"Hey, LuAnne."

Kate jumped at the sound of the raspy voice and turned to look for its source. Two men were parked in rickety wooden folding chairs against the far wall. Both held half-full bottles of RC Cola in their laps.

LuAnne waved a greeting. "How y'all doin', boys?"

Boys? Both of them looked like they could have come over on the ark. At the very least, they predated this decrepit building by a good many years.

"When's the diner gonna open up again?" called the wispy-haired old-timer on the left.

LuAnne shrugged. "You'll have to talk to Loretta about that, Walt. I'm not real sure what her plans are." She raised her voice. "Bernie, where are you? You got a minute to talk?"

A muffled grunt came from beneath the truck, and Kate watched a pair of coverall-clad legs emerge from under the near side, followed by a grimy torso, and finally a grease-smeared face that burst into a wide grin when he caught sight of the two women.

"I've always got time for my favorite waitress. What's up?"

"This is my friend, Kate Hanlon. She's our pastor's wife out at Faith Briar. Someplace you should consider visiting instead of sleepin' in on Sunday mornings."

Bernie pulled himself to his feet and extended his hand to Kate. Then, glancing down at his grease-encrusted palm, he appeared to think better of it and brought it back to his side.

He grinned at her instead. "What can I do for you? You need an oil change?"

Why did everyone seem bent on servicing her car? Kate eyed the onlookers in the back, who were obviously hanging on every word. She wondered if she and LuAnne should speak privately with Bernie in his office.

LuAnne, though, didn't seem to feel the least bit uncomfortable about having the old-timers listen in. Kate gave Bernie a bright smile.

"I'm just looking for some information today, and I wondered if you might be able to help me."

"Fire away."

"Do you know a man named Roland Myers?" She waited for the umpire to call strike three.

Bernie swiped at his cheek with a greasy rag, leaving behind a wide swath of black. "Lives out on Mountain Laurel? Sure, I know him."

"Do you ever buy any used parts from him?" She held her breath, hoping the question hadn't sounded accusatory.

Bernie's face took on a comical look of surprise. "Buy from him? No, but I sell him quite a few parts. At least, I used to."

He stuffed the rag back in his pocket. "He's always needin' something for those cars he restores. He doesn't have the cash to spring for brand-new parts, but I can usually find something we can jury-rig so it'll do the job for him."

His grin faded, and concern shadowed his features. "Come to think of it, I haven't seen him for a while. I hope he's okay."

Uh-oh. Had she just established herself as a friend of Roland's? "I, uh, saw him just the other day. He looked fine to me."

"Glad to hear it." Bernie stuck his hands in his back pockets and glanced at the truck he'd been working on. "Well, if that's all . . ."

Kate took the hint. "Thank you for your time. It was nice meeting you."

"You, too, Miz Hanlon." Bernie started to

turn away, then paused. "Hanlon . . . Are you the one I read about in the *Chronicle*? The lady whose wallet turned up in Roland's Mustang?"

Kate closed her eyes and nodded. She could see it now. That would be the way she would go down in Copper Mill history.

Bernie beamed at her. "So he finally got her up and goin'! How's she run?"

Kate felt her mouth drop open.

On the other side of the shop, Walt planted his hands on his knees and wobbled to his feet. "Ain't gonna run at all anymore, the way I heard it."

He shuffled across the concrete floor and peered at Kate through his thick bifocals. "So you're the one who drove 'er through the diner."

His companion creaked his way over to join them. "I bet Loretta is plenty mad at you, right?"

Walt elbowed his buddy in the ribs. "Nope. The story is they were in on it together. I hear Loretta had the place insured for plenty."

"You're both wrong." Bernie shook his head and spoke with a tone of authority. "The word around town is she's gonna sell out and let someone else open a new restaurant. I hear they're emptying it all out and gettin' ready to put in one of them fancy French places with starched napkins and a mayterdee to show you to your table."

"Sounds like big money there." A thin laugh wheezed from Walt's scrawny chest, and he jerked his thumb in Kate's direction. "I guess she really did Loretta some kind of favor by plowin' into the diner, didn't she?"

Kate gaped at them all like a fish out of water.

LuAnne planted one hand on her hip and raised the other to point a finger at the trio. "Shame on you! Y'all are worse than a bunch of old women when it comes to gossip."

Then she wheeled around and said to Kate, "Come on, darlin'. We've found out all we're goin' to here."

Kate followed her friend back to the Honda and sank gratefully into the driver's seat. Her tottery legs wouldn't have supported her one moment longer.

A string of incoherent sounds came out of her mouth before she could manage to form actual words. "Is that what they think? That *I* was driving that car?"

LuAnne shifted in the seat until they were face-to-face, then she took Kate's right hand in hers. Leaning forward, she stared directly into Kate's eyes.

"It doesn't matter what that bunch of old gossips is sayin'. They've got way too much time on their hands and don't have anything better to do than stick their noses in other people's business."

"But it does matter." Kate choked on the words, dangerously close to tears. "If they really believe that . . ."

LuAnne tightened her grip. "Listen to me, darlin'. The people who know you don't believe this is anything more than a lot of hooey. Loretta doesn't, and neither do I. None of your friends, or anybody with a lick of sense, would ever think that. Knowin' you, you'll use the skill God gave you to find out what really went on, and this whole thing will blow over in no time.

"Plus, you have friends in this town, and we're gonna do anything we can to shut down these rumors and let people know you didn't have anything to do with that accident. If we weren't out sleuthin' this afternoon, I'd be on the phone right now. But don't you fret. We're gonna figure this out."

I hope she's right, Kate mused after she dropped LuAnne off at her home. But at least some folks believed in her and her ability to find the answers to the puzzle.

She knew she had better find them soon if she hoped to clear her name.

Kate pulled into a parking space in front of Smith Street Gifts and sat for a moment to collect her thoughts.

At the other end of the block stood what was left of the Country Diner, the favorite gathering place for so many local residents. Its absence had left a hole in the community as gaping as the one in the front of the diner.

Walt's question pushed its way into the forefront of her mind. When *was* Loretta planning to reopen? She should have asked LuAnne while they were together instead of letting herself get sidetracked.

Kate looked for any sign of reconstruction, but with the heavy black tarps blanketing the storefront, the building looked just as dismal as it had the night she and Paul came to offer help . . . and walked straight into a nightmare instead.

Misgivings stirred within her. What if the diner didn't reopen? Or worse, what if Bernie was right and an upscale French restaurant opened in its place?

Was that the reason for the tarps covering the windows — so Loretta could clear the place out and prepare for the transfer of ownership in secret?

A lump formed in Kate's throat as she tried to imagine Copper Mill without the Country Diner. What a loss it would be!

And she would be held responsible, if the truth wasn't found.

But the truth would come to light. It *had* to.

Shaking off her gloomy thoughts, Kate reached for the cardboard box she had placed on the backseat before leaving home.

She carried the box inside the store, relaxing in its familiar clutter of souvenirs and trinkets. The rest of the world might be going crazy, but here, at least, she felt in her element.

Steve Smith, the gift shop's owner, whistled admiringly as he held the sun catchers up to the light one by one. "You have a rare ability, Kate. Even in a piece this small, your talent shines through." He grinned and winked. "No pun intended."

Kate chuckled. "I enjoy doing these small items for a change of pace, but I have to admit I'm itching to sink my teeth into something a little more complex."

Steve rubbed his hands together. "I'm glad to hear it. A fella from Cincinnati came through yesterday on his way to Atlanta. He saw some of your work and wondered if you'd be willing to do a fanlight to put over the front door of the new home he's building."

Kate gasped in delight. "Any special design? When does he want it? Did he specify a color scheme?"

Steve laughed and held up his hand to stave off the barrage of questions. "I told him I thought you'd say yes, so he gave me the dimensions he needs and said he'd leave the design to you. After looking at your other work, he felt sure he'll be pleased with anything you come up with."

A water scene, perhaps. Or maybe an abstract design? Kate's mind reeled with possibilities.

Steve's voice called her back to the present. "He's supposed to be back this way in another month or so, but he left his business card."

Steve produced a card from behind the counter and handed it to her. "He said you can call him on his cell phone if you have any questions."

Kate beamed. Finally something positive to focus on! She thanked Steve and tucked the card in her purse, already planning the things she would ask her new customer when she called him.

The freedom to develop her own design was all well and good, but the details he could provide about his home and interests would help her create a piece that would bring him joy for years.

What kind of theme was he looking for? Scenic? Geometric? What shades did he plan to use in the color scheme of his new home, and what direction would the fanlight face?

She left Steve hanging the new offerings where they would best catch the light in the front window of his store and hummed as she returned to her car, her steps lighter than they had been for days.

Her thumb was poised to press the Unlock button on her key remote when she paused, thoughts about the errant Mustang intruding on her happy plans. Making a quick decision, she pivoted and walked across the green to the town hall.

She trotted up the concrete steps and through the glass doors, then turned right into the section of the building that housed the sheriff's office.

Skip looked up from his desk when she entered, and a wary look crossed his face. "What can I do for you, Missus Hanlon?"

Frustration billowed up in Kate when she saw the reserve in his gaze. "I've been wondering something. Who reported the crash?" She held her breath while she waited for him to answer.

Skip twirled a pencil in his fingers, turning it end over end. "To tell you the truth, I'm not sure. I didn't take the call myself, but I know it was a woman. She hung up before the other deputy could get her name."

His eyes narrowed, and he looked straight at Kate. "It wasn't —"

"No, it wasn't." Immediately she regretted her snappish tone. "I'm sorry, Skip. This whole thing has just gotten beyond frustrating."

The redheaded deputy's cheeks rounded as he blew out a puff of air. "You can say that again." Then he drew himself up and resumed his official demeanor. "But we're working on it. We'll turn up a lead sooner or later."

"Later is what I'm afraid of." Kate left Skip to his paperwork and exited the building through the glass doors.

"I can't believe it. They don't seem to have made any progress at all." Kate pulled the empty flour canister from the cupboard and closed the door with more force than was necessary.

"To tell you the truth, Paul, I don't think they're even trying hard to find out who did it." She reached for a fresh bag of flour and plunked it down beside the canister. A puff of white dust floated into the air, then the tiny motes drifted down again, coating the counter's surface with a fine powder.

Paul dampened a dish cloth and swabbed it over the mess. "You have to admit, it isn't exactly a major crime wave." Amusement tinged his voice. "I'm sure they have more pressing matters to worry about at the moment. They'll get to it — or not — in good time."

Kate took the cloth from him and rinsed it out under the kitchen faucet. "I'm concerned about how this could impact our ministry here."

"I can't see how a missing wallet would have any effect on what happens at Faith Briar."

Kate wrung out the cloth and spread it across the sink divider. "That missing wallet of mine wound up in a stolen car, hon. I don't want people thinking I was somehow involved."

Paul burst out laughing. "Not involved? Who's the one who's always poking her nose into things and trying to solve every mystery that comes along?"

Kate poured the flour from the bag into the canister, careful not to repeat her earlier dusting. "But that's usually because I want to help someone else. It's a whole different feeling when it comes to solving a mystery on my own behalf."

And that was the problem, she thought as she rolled out the dough to make the crust for chocolate pecan pie.

It was one thing to try to sort out someone else's dilemma, using her God-given gifts to put the pieces of the puzzle together. But it was quite another to go through the day-to-day stress of knowing she would have to live with the repercussions of a tainted reputation if she didn't succeed.

Kate tried to explain that to Paul while they ate.

He listened until she had run out of words, then he covered her hand with his own. "Kate, you believe God is in control, don't you?"

She blinked at the question. "Of course."

"Then I think you need to just let go and let him take care of this. It isn't going to go away any faster with you stressing over it."

"I *am* trusting God." The corners of her lips tipped upward. "I just want to help clear things up."

Paul squeezed her fingers. "Honey, we have a fine sheriff in Alan Roberts. I'm sure he's giving the case all the attention it deserves. Just leave it to him and let him find the culprit."

He kissed her fingertips, then settled back in his chair. "Let's look at the worst-case scenario. Suppose they never do find who was behind this. What's the absolute worst thing that could happen?"

Kate stared into the distance, unwilling to put her deepest concerns into words.

Paul spread his hands. "In that case, it becomes an unsolved mystery. Those happen all the time. They make television shows about them, although this one probably wouldn't even make prime time."

He grinned and folded his arms, apparently satisfied with this flow of logic. "My point is, life goes on. God will deal with whoever did this in his good time, even if that person is never brought to earthly justice."

"I suppose you're right." Kate speared a green bean with her fork and pushed it around her plate. What if Paul's worst-case scenario came true and this went down in the annals of unsolved mysteries? Could she do what Paul suggested and just let it go?

She thought about the faces she'd seen around town since the accident, the faces of people she'd worked so hard to win over, now filled with suspicion. If she didn't find out what her wallet was doing in that stolen car, she might never regain their trust.

They would continue to look at her as though she were flaky at best, if not an outright criminal.

Worse, despite Paul's assurances to the contrary, the germs of distrust could spread to infect his ministry as well. How could people continue to trust him as a spiritual leader if he couldn't keep his deranged wife out of trouble?

Her thoughts tumbled over one another while she cleared their plates and dished up slices of the chocolate pecan pie.

After the first bite, Paul closed his eyes and sighed. "No doubt about it, that's a blue-ribbon recipe."

When he had savored the last bite and dabbed up the crumbs, he pushed the plate away and reached for her hand. "All joking aside, it was a fabulous meal. You do so many things well, Katie. You're a wonderful cook and a gifted artist. And you've been my main supporter and head cheerleader for all these years. Plus, you've already solved more than your share of mysteries since we've been in Copper Mill. God has given you a gift in that area as well."

He reached over and stroked her cheek.

"To put it in sports vernacular, nobody bats a thousand. Even if the identity of the car thief is never discovered, don't let one miss make you feel like a failure."

Kate nodded and smiled. "I guess you're right."

She thought about what he said while she cleaned up the kitchen. Paul was right. She had to trust God. If this mystery remained unsolved, it wouldn't make her a failure.

But that didn't mean she was going to quit trying.

Chapter Ten

"You're driving over to the game with me, aren't you?" Paul dropped his basketball shoes into his sports bag, then zipped it shut.

"Actually, I have a few errands I need to run."

When the expectant look on his face dimmed, Kate wrapped her arms around his waist and hastened to add, "But I'll be there, hon, never fear. I wouldn't miss the chance to watch you lead the Faith Briar team to victory."

Paul's grin returned as quickly as it had faded. "Confidence. A man likes to hear that from his wife." He picked up the bag and gave her a quick kiss. "I'll be watching for you."

Kate waved good-bye as he pulled out of their driveway, then she gathered her things and climbed into her Honda.

Paul always liked to get to the gym early,

before the others gathered to start warming up. She would only wind up standing around tapping her toes if she went with him. She would do better to put the extra time to good use.

She felt a twinge of guilt when she spotted his pickup in the high-school parking lot, and she eased off the gas.

How his face would light up if she postponed her errands and walked into the gym right then. None of her errands were crucial. It wouldn't hurt a bit to let them go until the following day.

But her hesitation lasted only an instant, then she pressed on the accelerator once more and continued toward town.

Her errands provided an excuse for going into town, but they weren't the real reason for her trip. She wanted — no, *needed* — to put her mind at rest, and as quickly as possible.

Betty Anderson looked up when Kate walked into the beauty parlor.

"Hey, there. I'm getting ready to give Lucy Mae a perm."

Betty gestured with the gray plastic perm rod in her hand to indicate the mayor's wife, seated in the salmon-colored chair in front of her.

"I've talked her into trying a curlier look. But I can work you in after that, if you don't mind sitting a bit. We can all visit while you wait."

"That's okay." Kate pulled her purse strap farther up on her shoulder and perched on the edge of one of the benches at the front of the shop. "I just wanted to ask you a quick question."

"Okay, shoot."

"Do you have any idea who made the call to report the crash at the diner to the sheriff's office?"

Kate held her breath. Most of the gossip in Copper Mill funneled through the beauty shop at some point. If there had been any talk, surely Betty would know about it.

Betty paused in the act of sliding end papers along a length of Lucy Mae's hair and looked at Kate oddly.

Kate squirmed. Okay, so maybe it was a dumb question. Aloud, she said, "Sorry, I just thought you might have heard something."

Betty kept staring at Kate. The end papers slipped from her fingers and fluttered downward, coming to rest on Lucy Mae's nose.

Lucy Mae sniffed and swatted them away, then she twisted in her seat to glare up at Betty.

Without shifting her gaze, Betty pulled out two more papers and positioned them around the section of hair again.

"I've heard plenty, but why would you be asking me? You should know all about it, seeing as how you were the one . . ."

Her voice trailed off, and she raised her carefully groomed eyebrows. "Weren't you?"

Kate clamped her teeth together and counted to ten. "I didn't make that call. I don't know how I lost my wallet, and I have no idea how it got into that car. I didn't know a thing about the crash until LuAnne called to tell me what happened."

Betty and Lucy Mae stared at her, their eyes wide.

Kate took a deep breath and tried to keep her voice steady. "Would you do me a favor? Next time someone comes in spreading that story, you can set them straight."

"Sure, Kate." Betty set the perm rod under the end papers and wound Lucy Mae's hair around it, looking thoughtful.

Kate stood, ready to leave, then paused at the door. "One more thing. Do either of you know a skinny boy, maybe fifteen or sixteen? He has sandy hair that keeps falling in his eyes, and he wears a brown leather jacket."

Betty and Lucy Mae exchanged glances,

then they both looked back at Kate and shrugged.

"Just thought I'd check." She attempted a laugh that didn't quite come off. "I bumped into him the other day and wondered who he was."

Kate glanced at her watch and winced. She hadn't meant to take so long at Betty's. If she didn't hurry, she'd never make it to the bank before it closed.

Knowing the parking spaces nearby would probably be taken up at this point on a Friday afternoon, she left her Honda in front of the beauty parlor and cut across the Town Green.

By the time she reached the bank, she was puffing. That would teach her to speed walk like someone trying out for the Olympics. She leaned against the brick facade long enough to catch her breath and massage her arthritic knee.

Maybe she needed to start working out more. She wasn't in nearly the condition Paul was. Healthy eating wouldn't do her much good if her body wasn't in shape.

Due to the prolonged cold snap, it had been a while since she and Livvy had taken one of their midday walks. Too long, obviously. Kate made a mental note to give

Livvy a call about starting up again.

A quick look at the clock tower at the southwest corner of the green jolted her into action again.

The plate-glass door of the Mid-Cumberland Bank and Trust opened before she could reach for the brass handle, and two men came out.

Kate drew to one side when she recognized one of them as Roland Myers. Myers, however, appeared lost in his own thoughts and didn't seem to notice Kate.

"No, McKinney turned me down again," he told his companion in a peevish voice. "I can't figure it. Haven't I lived in these parts all my life? How does he figure that makes me a poor credit risk?"

His voice trailed off as the two men walked away, and Kate hurried inside the bank. She took a moment to savor the fragrant aroma of the coffee Melvin McKinney, the bank manager, kept perking for his customers. If she weren't in such a hurry, she would have lingered long enough to help herself to a cup.

At the moment, though, she had more pressing matters to attend to. With a wistful sigh, she turned toward the tellers' counter on her left and waited in line until Georgia — or was it Evelyn? — Cline was free to help her. It was almost impossible to tell the elderly twins apart. They not only dressed alike, but they even wore their Easter-egg blue hair in the same style.

Behind her, she saw Melvin McKinney locking the door behind one of the last customers. She had gotten there not a moment too soon!

Kate darted a surreptitious glance at the teller's nameplate as she approached the counter.

"Hello, Georgia. I'm sorry for cutting it so near to closing time. I only need to make a deposit, though, so it won't take long." She pulled the check and deposit slip from her purse and slid them across the counter.

Georgia smiled and completed the transaction. "No problem, Mrs. Hanlon."

"It's always nice to see a cheerful face like yours at the end of the day," Evelyn chimed from her perch on the high stool next to her sister.

Kate smiled her thanks and reached for the receipt Georgia handed her, trying not to show her excitement at the idea that just popped into her mind. The Cline twins were usually willing to talk about almost anything. Perhaps she could use that to her advantage now.

Taking the time to fold the slip of paper

neatly in half before sliding it into her purse, she asked as casually as she could, "Do either of you know of a family who moved here recently? I don't know their last name, but they have a teenage son. He's very slender and seems to be a bit of a loner."

The sisters blinked at each other, then turned back to Kate and shook their heads in unison. "That doesn't ring a bell with me," Georgia said.

"Me, either." Evelyn scrunched up her lips. "Whereabouts do they live?"

Kate floundered, worried she had said too much. "I'm not sure. I don't know much about them, actually. It's just that I've met their son and . . ."

Evelyn bobbed her head as though Kate's query made perfect sense. "And being the pastor's wife, you want to welcome the newcomers to the community. If we hear anything about them, we'll let you know."

Kate drew in a grateful sigh. "That would be wonderful. I really would like to meet them." She moved toward the exit, where Melvin McKinney was waiting.

"Thank you for your business, Mrs. Hanlon." Ever the gentleman, he inclined his head in an old-fashioned bow, then turned the key in the lock with a flourish and opened the door wide.

Back outside, Kate hitched her purse strap up higher on her shoulder. With the last of her errands accomplished, she headed for the library.

Kate walked diagonally across the green and turned right on Main Street. The deep chime from the clock tower reminded her she had already taken far more time than she planned. If she didn't hurry, she would be late for Paul's game. Kate quickened her steps.

Was she being foolish for stopping to talk to Livvy now when they would see each other at the gym in only a short time? She tamped down her doubts and kept on walking. The gym was no place for a private discussion.

They wouldn't have much time to hash things over before they headed to the gym, but she felt a deep need to discuss the situation with her friend in a less chaotic setting. Livvy, with her organized mind, had a way of unsnarling the most tangled situations, something Kate desperately needed at this point.

A rush of warm air greeted Kate when she pushed through the library door. She glanced around the first floor. A quick peek behind the door bearing the title Head Librarian showed her that Livvy wasn't in her office, and Kate didn't spot her anywhere among the shelves of the fiction collection. She decided Livvy must be upstairs and made her way up the stairs.

Sure enough, Kate found her on the second floor, helping a patron get set up on one of the library's Internet computers.

Kate waggled her fingers to get her friend's attention, then she fidgeted while she waited for Livvy to finish with the patron. She could only see the back of the young man's head, but even from this angle he looked strangely familiar.

Curious, Kate studied him more closely: sandy hair and a scrawny frame . . . Her eyes widened when she recognized the boy she had just asked about at Betty's and the bank.

Kate ducked inside one of the private meeting rooms, not wanting her presence to make him uncomfortable. She slipped off her coat and hung it on the back of the nearest chair. A moment later, Livvy joined her.

"It's good to see you!" she exclaimed, giving Kate a quick hug. "I missed two days of work trying to fight off that cold, and I've been scrambling to catch up ever since. I can't believe we haven't had a chance to talk this week."

"I've missed you too." Kate stared out through the doorway. "That boy, Livvy. The one you were helping on the computer. Who is he?"

Livvy shrugged. "I really don't know much about him. He hasn't been around town long. He stops in occasionally to use the computer, but he doesn't talk much. Why?"

Kate shrugged. "Just being nosy, I guess. It really doesn't matter."

She hadn't lost her desire to learn more about the teenager, but that would have to wait until she had more time to satisfy her curiosity. At the moment, she had other priorities.

"I can't stay long, but I wanted to talk some more about what happened at the diner. Do you have a few minutes?"

Without hesitation, Livvy closed the meeting-room door. Her hazel eyes took on a sympathetic gleam, and she rested her hand on Kate's arm.

"Are you doing okay?"

Kate started to shake her head, then nodded, unable to speak for the sudden tightening in her throat. She swallowed hard, then continued.

"It's so frustrating! People are talking about me all over town, and you wouldn't believe the stories they're telling. I'm worried about losing the ground we've gained here. We've worked so hard, and now to watch it all slip away . . ."

"Don't go jumping to conclusions, Kate Hanlon." Livvy tilted her head and took on the stern expression Kate thought of as her "librarian look."

"You've never been a quitter as long as I've known you, and this is no time to start. There's an answer to all this; we just have to find out what it is."

Livvy leaned against the long table in the center of the room and folded her arms, as if she had all the time in the world to listen. "Start at the beginning and tell me what you know."

Kate related the events of the previous week, starting with LuAnne's late-night call. Her voice cracked when she got to the part about going to the sheriff's office to pick up her wallet.

"He had Skip *fingerprint* me, Livvy. Like some kind of criminal. Can you believe it?" The stunned expression on Livvy's face was balm to her wounded feelings.

"People were already acting funny while we were helping clean up at the diner that night. But since the news article came out . . ."

She took the tissue Livvy pressed into her hand and dabbed at her eyes.

"I'm sorry. The last thing I want to do right now is fall apart. What I really need is to find out the truth so I can put this whole nightmare behind me."

"You're absolutely right." Livvy's brisk tone was like a refreshing breeze, sweeping away the cobwebs of self-pity. "So let's figure this out. How do you think your wallet got inside that Mustang?"

Kate shook off the despair that question always brought. This was no time to wallow in confusion; this was the time to go on the offensive. She tossed the tissue into the wastebasket and squared her shoulders.

"I've asked myself the same question over and over, and I have no idea. None at all."

"All right." Livvy tapped one finger against her cheek. "Let's go back over what you did that Wednesday. Do you remember where you were and who you were with?"

Kate nodded. She had gone over those details so many times, they rolled off her tongue almost without having to think about them.

"I worked in my studio all morning and ran errands most of the afternoon. First, I stopped by the Mercantile to pick up a few things for supper. Then I had my nails done at Betty's."

Livvy nodded. "So far, so good. What else?"

"I checked in at Smith Street Gifts to see if any of my pieces had sold. They hadn't," she added, crinkling her nose.

Livvy's eyes twinkled. "You can forget about making a bid for my sympathy. You're a wonder with stained glass, and you know it. Now get back on track. Did you do anything else in town that day?"

"I stopped here. That was the day we were talking about the herb garden I want to put in this spring. You suggested a couple of books, remember?"

Livvy nodded. "What did you do then?"

"I went home." Kate spread her hands wide, feeling as helpless as she did every time she went over her activities that fateful day.

"I fixed supper and then went to choir practice. When I got back, Paul wanted to tell me about some new strategy he and Danny were working on for the next game. We went to bed around ten, and the next thing I knew, the phone started ringing and kicked this whole crazy melodrama into motion."

Livvy trailed her forefinger along the edge of the table. "So, when did your wallet go missing?"

"That's the big question, isn't it? I have absolutely no idea."

Livvy stirred uneasily. "I hate to think of anything like this, but is it possible you and Paul had a break-in and didn't realize it? Maybe the wallet was missing before you ever left the house."

Kate shook her head. "I had my purse with me the whole time I was in town. That's what makes this whole thing seem so impossible. It simply couldn't have happened. But it did."

She let out a nervous laugh. "All I can think is that someone stole the wallet right from under my nose, but that isn't exactly a comforting thought."

"No . . ." Livvy drew the word out slowly. "And I can't imagine it happening in any of those places. Betty's Beauty Parlor? Sam Gorman's Mercantile? Smith Street Gifts?"

She looked over her shoulder in a melodramatic fashion and lowered her voice to a whisper. "Or how about right here at the Copper Mill Public Library, a well-known haunt for sneak thieves?"

Kate couldn't help laughing at her friend's antics. "All right, point taken. But that just leaves us back where we started."

"Not necessarily. Why don't we look on

the bright side? Let's say your wallet slipped out of your purse after you left here. Someone found it and planned to be a good Samaritan and return it to you."

Kate shook her head. "And that same someone drove Roland Myers' car through Loretta's diner and then left the scene? That doesn't seem very good Samaritan-like, does it?"

"You have a point." Livvy sighed and looked at the clock on the wall. "Why don't we keep talking while I get my purse and lock my office? Then I'll follow you over to the gym."

Kate glanced at her watch and flinched when she realized how much time had slipped away. Paul's game was about to begin!

She snatched up her coat. "Thanks, but I've got to run. I promised Paul I'd be there for the start of the game. He'll be wondering where I am. I'll go on ahead and save you a seat."

She had one arm in her coat sleeve and was reaching for the other when her cell phone started ringing. Kate dug it out of her purse and glanced at the Caller ID. "It's Paul."

Livvy grinned, shook her finger in a shame-on-you gesture, and mouthed,

"Busted."

Kate wrinkled her nose at her friend and scooped the phone from its pocket on one side of her purse. Feeling like a schoolgirl caught playing hooky, she pressed the button to receive the call, an apology forming on her lips.

"Hi, honey. I know I'm late, and I'm sorry. I'll be there in —"

"Kate?"

She frowned at the unexpected voice. "Hello? Who is this?"

"It's Danny Jenner. Paul told me to use his phone to call you."

Kate tucked the phone between her shoulder and her ear while she shoved her other arm into her coat sleeve. "Would you please tell him I'm sorry to be late? I'm on my way to the gym right —"

"Paul's been hurt. They've called an ambulance."

Kate pressed her hand to her chest and dropped into the nearest chair. "What's wrong? How did it happen?"

Livvy hurried over and knelt by her side. "What is it?"

"It's Danny," Kate whispered. "He says Paul is hurt." She tuned back in to what Danny was saying.

"— going up for a rebound during

warm-up and got tangled up with Jeff Turner. He must have come down on it at a bad angle. I don't think it's too serious, but they didn't want to take any chances."

Kate had to force herself to breathe. "I'll be there in five minutes."

"The ambulance is getting ready to pull out right now. That's why Paul wanted me to call you. You might as well head straight to Pine Ridge and meet them at the hospital."

Chapter Eleven

Kate rushed into the emergency-room entrance of the squat brick hospital. Guilt threatened to choke her like a hand around her throat.

Why hadn't she gone to the gym with Paul? Bad enough to be running so late in the first place, but not to be there when he was injured? *Unthinkable.*

The dark-haired secretary at the desk looked up and gave her a compassionate smile. "May I help you?"

"Paul Hanlon. They brought him in by ambulance just a little while ago. May I see him?"

"And you are . . . ?"

"His wife."

The secretary summoned a nurse who smiled and gestured toward the large double doors. "Come on back. I'll take you to him."

Kate followed her down a short corridor that ended in a series of cubicles. The nurse stopped at the last one and pushed back the curtain.

The sight of Paul lying on the narrow bed, his face nearly as pale as the crisp white sheets, proved to be her undoing. Kate rushed to his side and took his hand, trying to fight back her tears.

This was no time to fall apart, she admonished herself. He needed support, not a weepy wife.

"Hi, honey. I'm sorry I wasn't there." The words came out calmly enough, but remorse wrenched at her heart.

I wasn't there. The phrase echoed through her mind. He had supported her at every turn, and she wasn't there when he needed her.

Paul gave her fingers a gentle squeeze. "I learned something tonight. I'm not Superman."

Kate smiled at his attempt to make light of the situation, but she could see the pain that shadowed his eyes.

"Have they given you any medication?"

He shook his head. "Not until they find out whether I'll need surgery."

Kate brushed his hair away from his eyes, smoothing the salt-and-pepper strands back over his forehead. A blue plastic chair sat in the corner of the cubicle, and Kate pulled it closer to the bed. She settled into it, prepared for a long wait.

To her surprise, a woman in pale blue scrubs stepped into the cubicle almost immediately.

"Mr. Hanlon?" She consulted the chart in her hand. "Sorry. Reverend Hanlon. They're ready for you in X-ray." She unlocked the brake on the wheels of the bed and rolled it into the corridor.

Kate dropped a kiss on his forehead and turned to the nurse. "I'll be out in the waiting room."

Giving Paul's hand another squeeze, she fled to the sanctuary of the waiting room, glad she didn't have to spend one more minute confined in that cramped space.

A sea of concerned faces greeted her as she burst through the double doors into the waiting room. A dozen voices spoke at once.

"How's Pastor Paul?"

"Is his ankle broken?"

"Is he going to be all right?"

Kate skidded to a halt and took in the sight before her. The waiting room was packed with people, many of them wearing jackets over basketball jerseys, and all of them looking her way.

Pastor Bobby Evans from First Baptist walked up and took her by the hand. "We decided to postpone the game. It just didn't seem right to go on playing, knowing Paul's hurt. When I announced it and said I'd be coming over here, both teams wanted to come too."

He glanced around at the crowd and grinned. "Looks like most of the fans came along as well."

Kate looked at the faces, some from Faith Briar, others she recognized from First Baptist, Copper Mill Presbyterian, and St. Lucy's Episcopal, all of them showing genuine concern. Tears stung her eyes, and her vision misted.

"Thank you all for coming," she managed to say before her voice broke. How could she have felt alone when so many compassionate hearts existed in Copper Mill?

Danny Jenner stepped forward and ran his fingers through his dark, curly hair. "We want Paul to know we'll be here for him. And you," he added with a warm smile.

"Would you like us to stay and keep you company?" Pastor Bobby asked. "Not all of us, though." He surveyed the group and chuckled. "I get the feeling the secretary would be much happier if the waiting-room crowd thinned out a bit."

Kate swallowed hard before she could speak. "I'll be fine, but thank you."

She raised her voice so the whole gathering could hear. "Thank you so much for coming. I know it will mean as much to Paul as it does to me. They just took him back to X-ray, but we'll keep you posted when we know what's going on. In the meantime, please keep Paul in your prayers."

"Why don't we do that right now?" Pastor Bobby signaled the group to join hands and form a circle, then he led them in a prayer for Paul's quick recovery and strength for Kate during this time.

After the "Amen," Kate watched the well-wishers disperse, for once grateful for the speed and efficiency of the small-town grapevine.

When the last visitor had straggled out to the parking lot, Kate turned back to the waiting room. She wiggled her fingers at the secretary, who looked relieved at the mass departure.

A security guard walked in and took up a post along the wall nearest the door. Kate smiled at him, glad the secretary hadn't felt it necessary to call upon him to help their visitors on their way.

None of the padded chairs around the room looked particularly inviting. She settled on one that faced the double doors, wanting to know the moment the nurse emerged, bearing news of Paul.

The wind brushed icy fingers over the back of her neck when the outer door opened. Kate turned up the collar of her coat and reached for a magazine. Her hand froze when a cloud of Estée Lauder's Youth-Dew settled over her.

"Yoo-hoo! I was afraid you'd be sitting here all by yourself. I've come to keep you company."

The magazine slipped from Kate's fingers, and she summoned a weak smile. "Hello, Renee."

Renee Lambert swept around the row of chairs and seated herself next to Kate like a queen bestowing a favor on a subject. She propped her oversized Gucci bag on the empty chair beside her with care.

"I got a phone call from the prayer chain to tell me about Paul, and I rushed right over." Her fingers closed around Kate's arm, and she lowered her voice to a husky whisper. "It's his heart, isn't it?"

"What? Goodness, no. He hurt his ankle playing basketball. Didn't the prayer chain get that straight?"

Renee examined the polish on her freshly manicured nails. "Stories have a way of changing once they start making the rounds.

Sometimes it's hard to know just what the truth really is."

She unbuttoned her leopard-print coat and fanned herself. "You must admit it would be reasonable to assume it was his heart. After all, when men of a certain age go cavorting on a basketball court, trying to keep up with men many years their junior —"

"It's his ankle, Renee. Only his ankle." Kate put all the firmness she could into the statement.

Renee nodded, unperturbed. "Even in a minor crisis, it isn't good to be alone. Others may abandon you, but I know how to do my duty."

"I haven't exactly been abandoned. The whole team — both teams, actually — came down to check on him earlier, along with a lot of the fans. I told them I would be perfectly fine here alone."

She cast a sidelong glance at the older woman, hoping she would take the hint.

True to form, Renee chose not to notice. She looked around as if hoping for more drama — or at least a bigger audience.

Apparently giving up on the dramatic possibilities, she turned back to Kate. "What a week we've had! It's as though the whole community has been cursed with a string of bad luck."

"There's no such thing as luck," Kate reminded her.

Renee waved away the remark. "You have to admit it seems that Copper Mill has endured more than its share of unfortunate happenings lately. Poor Loretta, having to deal with all that mess. And now this."

She heaved a sigh in true drama-queen fashion. *Scarlett O'Hara would have approved,* Kate thought.

"And it can't have been an easy week for you, trying to explain what your wallet was doing in that car."

Kate clamped her lips together. No way was she going to be drawn into a discussion on *that* subject when her attention was focused on Paul.

"It seems so odd about the driver going missing," Renee went on. "Doesn't it seem strange to you that he — or she — would be able to just walk away like that? I wouldn't think it possible, considering the amount of damage that was done."

She sighed again. "But I guess there's only one person who knows what the real story is." She leaned over and purred, "You wouldn't know more about it than you've let on, would you?"

Kate sputtered. "Really, Renee! That is utterly ridiculous."

Renee settled back in her seat with a smug smile, as though her suspicions had just been confirmed.

Kate opened her mouth to add more when she saw Renee's Gucci bag move.

"Renee . . ."

"Yes?" The older woman moved slightly to her right and draped one arm around the bag, then looked at Kate with guileless eyes. The effect was spoiled when a whimper emanated from within the bag.

Kate bit her lip and tried not to laugh. "You brought Kisses in here, didn't you?"

Renee's eyes took on a stony glint. "And why shouldn't I? You don't think I'd leave my Little Umpkins out in the car on a cold night like this, do you?"

She opened the top of the bag just enough to slip her fingers inside. "There, now, Little Snuggle Umpkins. Mama's right here."

The whimpers increased in volume, then grew into a series of yips. The security guard detached himself from his post in the corner and strolled their way.

"Evenin' ladies." He nodded at Kate, then turned an implacable gaze on Renee.

"Miz Lambert, you know the rules. We don't allow dogs in the hospital."

"What dog?" Renee batted her improbably long eyelashes and assumed an air of innocence.

"The one in that bag." The guard hooked his thumbs in his belt and showed no signs of backing down.

"This bag?" Renee must have known she was waging a losing battle, but she wasn't about to admit it. The fighting spirit of the South lived on.

Unfortunately, Kisses chose that moment to bark at the top of his tiny voice. The guard rocked back on his heels. "No dogs allowed," he repeated.

Renee got to her feet and pulled the bag into her arms. "It's a sad day when a person can't come here to comfort a friend."

Her high heels clacked across the floor as she swept out of the emergency room.

Kate cast a grateful look at the security guard and picked up her magazine again. Surely it wouldn't be too much longer before she had some news.

Just then the double doors swung open, and Kate leaped to her feet. The nurse looked past her and motioned to a young woman holding a whimpering toddler. Kate sighed, then eased back into her seat again and resumed reading.

CHAPTER TWELVE

Kate had finished all the women's magazines she could find and was halfway through an article on marine ecology in the Caribbean when Dr. McLaughlin came out to talk to her. Kate rose and walked over to meet him.

"It's a fracture, all right." The lanky ER doctor pushed a thatch of dark hair back from his forehead. "The good news is that it won't require surgery. We're going to get him fixed up and send him home."

"How much longer?" The question slipped out before she could stop herself.

She could have bitten her tongue when she saw the exhaustion on the doctor's face. "I'm sorry. I don't mean to be impatient. It's just that . . ."

Dr. McLaughlin managed a smile despite his obvious weariness. "I know it's hard to sit out here and not be able to do anything but wait. Have you perused our fascinating reading material?" he joked. Kate laughed and gestured at the pile of magazines by her chair.

"We need to set the bone and get it stabilized. Barring any other emergencies, I should be finished with him in an hour or so." The doctor patted her arm and left to tend to Paul.

Kate took her seat again and glanced at her watch. If all went well, they might be getting into bed by ten thirty or so. She picked up the magazine she'd been reading and prepared to learn more about the fragile ecosystem of the coral reefs.

The scream of a siren split the night, and an ambulance backed up to the emergency entrance. The secretary called for an orderly, who hurried out into the cold night and helped a pair of EMTs bring in a man on a gurney.

A woman about Renee's age followed, weeping. She started to follow the procession into the back, but the secretary put a hand on her shoulder.

"Why don't you wait out here? Someone will be out to talk to you as soon as we know something."

The woman stared around the room as if unsure of what she was supposed to do. She let out a sob, then crumpled into the nearest chair and buried her face in her hands.

The woman's despair tore at Kate's heart. Laying her magazine aside, Kate crossed the room and knelt beside the sobbing woman.

"My name is Kate Hanlon, and my husband is a pastor in Copper Mill. Is there anything I can do to help?"

The woman's shoulders heaved several times before she raised her head. "I'm Eppie Barlow. They just brought my husband here in an ambulance."

Kate nodded. "I saw."

"We were playing canasta when Alvin turned pale and grabbed his left arm." Mrs. Barlow shuddered. "They think he may be having a heart attack."

"I'm so sorry." Kate took the other woman's hands in hers. "Would you like me to pray with you?"

Mrs. Barlow nodded. But before they could bow their heads, the double doors to the exam rooms burst open, and both women sprang to their feet.

A nurse scanned the room and beckoned to the older woman. "You can come back now. The doctor would like to speak with you."

Mrs. Barlow hurried to join the nurse. Just before she reached the door, she turned back to Kate. "I need to be with Alvin now, but would you please pray anyway?"

"Of course." Kate sat down again and lifted the Barlows up to her heavenly Father, adding a prayer of thanks for her own situation while she was at it.

There were far worse things to deal with than a broken ankle.

An hour later, Kate felt like she must have read the print off all the magazines in the waiting room.

How much longer?

Since Mr. Barlow had been brought in, two other emergency patients had arrived, each taking precedence over Paul's injury. She drummed her fingers on the arm of the padded chair. Maybe she could start counting the acoustic tiles in the ceiling.

She stretched her arms over her head and rolled her neck from side to side. Who would have thought just sitting could be so exhausting? Even Renee's company would be welcome now.

Maybe.

Did Kate really want to listen to more veiled comments about the identity of the Mustang's driver? She thumbed through a worn copy of a gardening magazine, wondering if she could find anything else of interest.

One of Renee's comments teased at the back of her mind, vying for her attention as she skimmed through an article on building worm beds.

Kate closed the magazine, her interest in friendly earthworms forgotten. What was it Renee said? She shut her eyes, the better to concentrate.

There had been the questions about Paul's heart and the pointed remarks about his age. Then the shift to Kate's least favorite subject of the moment, the diner-destroying Mustang. After that . . .

Kate pressed her fingers against her eyelids. What happened then?

After that, Kisses made his presence known, followed by Renee's grand exit. But there had been something else, she just knew it. Something about the Mustang . . . No, not the Mustang, but its driver.

Kate's eyelids flew open. Of course! Renee's oh-so-casual comment about the driver being able to walk away from the accident.

More than one person had expressed surprise that the driver had escaped the scene without injury. But had he really been unhurt?

Kate crossed the tile floor and stood at

the desk. The new secretary — there had been a shift change at 10:00 p.m. — looked up inquiringly.

"I was wondering, could you tell me whether someone came in here last week on Wednesday night?"

The woman's face registered disbelief. "This is an emergency room. People come in here all the time."

Kate pressed her lips together. That hadn't come out right at all. "It would have been quite late."

The secretary thawed a bit. "I'm on the late shift most Wednesdays, but there are always a lot of patients."

"Or it might have been very early Thursday morning. In the middle of the night, anyway. Not with an illness but an injury. Something that might have come from an auto accident." Kate held her breath and hoped for the best.

"That's interesting." The other woman leaned on her elbows and looked directly at Kate. "The sheriff came in here last week and asked the same question."

"Oh?" She should have known this was a bad idea. "What a coincidence."

The secretary drew herself up. "You realize, of course, that the Patient Privacy Act prohibits me from divulging information of that kind."

Kate felt her face flame. "Of course. I shouldn't have bothered you."

"Except . . ." — the secretary leaned toward Kate and lowered her voice to a conspiratorial whisper — "that only applies if there *was* a patient. I guess it's okay to tell you there wasn't anyone who fit that description."

She grinned and settled herself back in her chair. "As a matter of fact, that shift was unusually slow. We only had a couple of patients all night."

"Oh well, thank you. I guess that answers my question."

"Happy to help." The phone rang, and the woman turned to answer it.

Kate slunk back to her seat, hoping news of her attempt to extract information didn't get back to Sheriff Roberts. So much for her bright idea of looking for a person with a mysterious limp.

After what seemed like an eternity, the doors to the exam rooms swung open again, and Paul appeared, seated in a wheelchair pushed by a husky male nurse.

Kate hurried over to him, taking in his drawn appearance and the large black contraption on his right leg. A pair of crutches lay across the arms of the wheelchair.

"It's called a moon boot," he told her. "Quite the fashion accessory, isn't it? They gave me a choice between black and gray. I thought black would look more dignified for Sundays." He attempted a smile in spite of the strain that showed on his face.

Following his lead, Kate swallowed back a sympathetic comment and kept her tone light. "So you're ready to leave?"

"He's all set," the nurse said. "If you'll pull your car up to the door, I'll wheel him out."

Bringing the car around was one thing; loading Paul into it was quite another. First, the crutches went into the backseat, then Kate had to push the passenger seat back as far as it would go to accommodate his outstretched leg.

The muscular nurse helped Paul stand, pivot, and finally maneuver himself inside the car.

"Nice job," the nurse said, pulling the wheelchair away from the car. He handed a small bottle and a slip of paper to Kate. "These are his pain pills. The directions are on the label. It's just a sample, though. You'll have to have the prescription filled at your local pharmacy if he needs more."

Kate thanked the nurse, tucked the pills and the prescription inside her purse, and went around to the driver's side. "That was quite a performance."

Paul let his head rest against the back of the seat and closed his eyes. "Wait until you see my next number. That's the real show-stopper."

Kate turned the key in the ignition, doing her best to keep up a cheerful front, all the while wondering how on earth she was going to get him inside the house on her own once they got home.

Chapter Thirteen

A shaft of sunshine found its way through a crack in the bedroom curtains and hit Kate square in the face. She scrunched her eyes closed and rolled over, pulling the blanket partway over her head.

Paul moaned softly, and Kate came fully awake. Turning her head with care so as not to wake him, she saw that his eyes were closed. She lay still for a moment, watching his chest rise and fall in a gentle rhythm.

Easing the covers back, she slipped out of bed as quietly as she could, then put on her robe and slippers and tiptoed out to the living room.

She went through the motions of grinding fresh coffee beans, then leaned against the counter while the coffee machine did its work. After being up late the night before and sleeping longer than usual that morning, she felt more than ready for her first sip by the time the coffee was finished brewing.

When the last drop had dripped through the filter, she filled a blue flowered mug, then wandered out to the living room, where she curled up in her favorite rocking chair with her Bible on her lap.

The fragrant steam wafted up from her mug, its rich aroma tantalizing her taste buds. She took a long sip of the dark brew and felt the caffeine begin to jolt her awake. Maybe she could make it through the day after all.

Kate brushed her fingers across the cover of her Bible. Of course she could make it through the day, and it had nothing to do with a caffeine surge.

Kate opened her Bible to the place where she had ended her reading the day before, in the ninth chapter of Mark. She started chapter ten, sipping from her mug and letting her mind absorb the message.

The story of Jesus inviting the little children to come to him always brought joy to her heart. She continued through the passage about the rich young man and then moved on to James and John's request for special honor.

"If only they had known what they were

asking," she murmured as she turned the page.

The words at the top of the column riveted her attention. *For even the Son of Man did not come to be served, but to serve, and to give his life as a ransom for many.*

She cradled the Bible in her lap and leaned her head back against the rocker, letting her eyelids drift closed.

What a reminder! When she helped Paul in from the car the night before, their awkward progress across the garage and through the house made her keenly aware of how dependent on her he would be, for the time being at least.

How was she going to cope? Already she was wondering if she had bitten off more than she could chew with that special order from the gift shop. She would need to spend every moment she could in her studio if she hoped to finish the fanlight in the time she had indicated.

On top of that, she needed to find out who was responsible for the theft of the Mustang and why Roland Myers wasn't all that concerned about getting it back. This disruption in her life couldn't have come at a worse time.

Her eyes flew open. What was she thinking, complaining about her own inconvenience when Paul was the one who was injured and in pain?

Lord, forgive me for my self-centeredness. You have blessed me in so many wonderful ways, yet all I seem to be able to do lately is focus on the negative. Give me a spirit of servanthood and a willingness to put others before myself.

Easier said than done. It was simple enough to talk about serving others, but now that she had the opportunity to put it into practice . . . But she would do it, with God's help. And she would do it with a joyful attitude.

A clicking noise caught her attention, and she looked up to see Paul enter the living room. He moved stiffly on his crutches, looking uncharacteristically vulnerable. Kate jumped up and ran to help him.

"Just call me Hopalong Cassidy," he quipped.

His face was still drawn and pale, but at least his outlook was cheerful. With short, jerky movements, he headed to the kitchen table and tried to scoot his usual chair back with the tip of one crutch.

Kate's heart swelled at his determination not to let this injury get the best of him. Since the moment she fell in love with him, she always said she would do anything for this man. Here was another opportunity to prove it.

She pulled the chair away from the table and steadied him as he sat down. "What can I get you to eat?"

"Believe it or not, I'm not too hungry, even after missing supper last night."

Kate wrinkled her nose. Until that very moment, she hadn't even thought about having missed their evening meal. She must have been even more tired than she thought. No wonder she had overslept.

"I think I'll just have a cup of coffee to start and then see if I want anything else later on."

Kate poured him a mug, then carried it to the table and slid her chair next to his. "Tell me what I can do for you."

Paul laughed. "I'm really not as fragile as all that. You don't have to watch me as if I'm going to shatter at any moment."

He reached out to her, and she moved inside the circle of his arm.

"I'm going to be fine, Katie. Don't you worry. In a matter of weeks, this will all be behind us, and then I'll be up and around again. This will be my chance to see how well I can learn to be content in any circumstance."

He planted a kiss behind her left ear and

squeezed her tight. "There, now. Does that feel like the hug of an invalid?"

Kate laughed with him, as much from relief as from his cheesy attempt at humor. "All right, I'll quit hovering over you. But face it, you aren't going to be able to jump up every time you need something. Is there anything I can get for you right now?"

"My Bible, my commentary, and my notepad," Paul answered without hesitation. "I need to work on my sermon."

Kate crossed her arms and gave him a stern look. "You're not planning to preach tomorrow, are you?"

"It's only my ankle that's injured, remember? My mind and my voice are just fine."

"And just how do you plan to get up the stairs and onto the platform? Just getting in and out of the car last night . . ."

Her voice trailed off. Had she forgotten her intention to serve so quickly? She had to do better than that. After a moment's thought, she offered, "Why don't I call Eli Weston? Maybe he can help."

"What a brilliant idea." Paul grinned at her. "That's why I already called him from the bedroom phone."

He laughed and ducked his head to one side when Kate swatted at him. "He'll be over tomorrow in plenty of time to give me a hand getting inside the church and up to the pulpit.

"If I need it, that is." He bounced one of the crutches' rubber tips against the floor. "I'm doing pretty well on these things already. By tomorrow I expect to be an old hand at this."

Kate laughed and started to relax for the first time since getting Danny's phone call.

Paul was right. This would be nothing more than a minor inconvenience after all. There was no point in getting in a dither over what couldn't be changed.

She made a mental list of errands she needed to do: a trip to the Mercantile, a stop at the dry cleaner's to pick up Paul's suit, then a visit to the pharmacy on Ashland Street to fill his prescription for pain pills.

If Paul promised to behave himself, she could get those things taken care of before lunch and spend the afternoon sketching possible designs for the fanlight. After Steve gave her the order, she had spoken to Harry Michaels, the customer from Cincinnati, and she already had several ideas she wanted to get down on paper before they slipped away.

Lost in her thoughts, it took a moment to realize that Paul was speaking. "What did you say?"

"I just asked if you would mind doing me a favor."

Ah, another chance to practice servanthood. "Of course! What is it?"

"After the lecture I got from Old Man Parsons and Renee — and from a number of others as well — I want to make sure there isn't any reason for them to criticize Avery's work tomorrow."

Paul ran his hand across his jaw. "He's supposed to clean the church on Fridays, so I planned to stop by this morning to make sure everything is in order before tomorrow's service. Would you mind taking care of that for me?

"Or," he added with a twinkle in his eye, "I could hobble out to my truck and drive over there myself."

"Don't even think about that! I have errands to run anyway. I'll stop there on my way into town. It shouldn't take more than a few minutes."

"Thanks, honey. I appreciate it." A crease appeared between Paul's eyebrows. "I really don't want Avery to know I'm checking up on him. He's just beginning to get some of his confidence back, and I don't want to do anything to undermine that."

He shifted his leg to a more comfortable

position. "I know the man has failed in the past, but I truly believe he's committed to turning his life around this time. And I mean to see he gets that second chance."

Kate stroked his cheek with her fingertips. "You're a good man, Paul Hanlon. Do you know that?"

Paul shook his head. "Not good; just grateful. God has extended grace to me. I just want to do the same for others."

An hour later, after making Paul comfortable on the couch and placing pillows under his foot, Kate set off for town. She headed south on Smoky Mountain Road and made a left turn on Mountain Laurel, mentally running through the list of things she needed to get done that morning.

She pulled into the church parking lot and sat for a moment, struck as always by the church's simple beauty, with its clean white lines and the steeple that seemed to point the way to heaven itself. A praise song popped into her mind, and she sang the words softly.

Life was good. Maybe it wasn't going quite the way she expected it to at the moment, but from now on she would adopt Paul's attitude as her own and learn to find contentment in every circumstance.

But sitting in the car wasn't going to get anything done. Still singing under her breath, she pulled her key ring from the Honda's ignition, climbed out of the car, and crossed the gravel lot to let herself in through the front door.

She stepped into the foyer, ready to give the building a cursory examination, her mind already moving ahead to the other errands she had to do.

Two steps past the door, the song died on her lips.

On her right, the door to the ladies' restroom stood ajar. Kate could see the mess of paper towels spilling over the top of the trash basket from where she stood.

Closer inspection showed a spattered mirror and commodes that obviously hadn't been cleaned since the previous Sunday. The men's room on the other side of the foyer was in even worse condition.

"What on earth?" Kate's involuntary question bounced off the plain white walls.

Wondering what she would find next, she moved into the sanctuary and stopped just inside the large double doors. Bulletins littered the oak pews, and the maple floorboards were covered with dust.

Kate walked down the broad center aisle toward the pulpit, noting more disarray with every step she took. It didn't look like anything at all had been done in the way of cleaning. The church was nowhere near ready for people to walk in and worship in the morning.

She ran both hands through her hair. What could Avery have been thinking?

Before her temper got the best of her, Kate took a moment to send up a quick prayer for patience. Maybe she was jumping to conclusions. Maybe Avery cleaned the downstairs first and got called away before he could finish.

Yes, that must have been it. She turned back to the foyer and started down the stairs to the basement. It couldn't be this bad everywhere.

She was wrong. The basement was even worse.

Kate held on to the stair railing for support while she surveyed the multipurpose room that served as a gathering place for meetings and potlucks.

Remnants of crafts done during Thursday's Mother's Day Out were still in evidence, from the tiny bits of paper scattered across the floor to the patches of dried glue on the long folding tables.

Kate peeked into the Sunday-school classrooms, then the kitchen. Still no sign of Avery.

With a sinking feeling, she recalled what Renee had said the Sunday before. Avery had fallen off the wagon more than once. Was she right? Was Avery at home even now, nursing a hangover?

Kate charged back up the stairs. Hangover or not, the man had a job to do, and he was going to do it.

She made her way to Paul's office and reached for the phone, then realized she didn't know Avery's number. A quick search of Paul's desk didn't turn up the information she needed. Kate tapped her fingernails on the desk blotter. She didn't want to call Paul and upset him, but she needed to find that number.

"Millie!" The obvious answer popped into Kate's mind like a lightbulb going off over a cartoon character's head.

She should have thought of Millie right away. The church secretary knew every detail of everything that went on at Faith Briar. She'd probably already committed Avery's number to memory. Kate could ask for it without offering any explanation. Paul wouldn't want her to give Millie another reason to criticize Avery.

With a rising sense of hope, Kate tapped

in Millie's home number. The secretary's curt "Hello" came through the receiver after the first ring.

"Millie, this is Kate Hanlon. I'm down at the church —"

"And you're wondering why the place is a total mess." Millie's crisp tone sounded even more clipped than usual. "Don't expect me to take the blame for that. I told the pastor he should never have hired that ne'er-do-well. I knew it would only be a matter of time before he slacked off on the job and caused trouble."

Kate's grip on the receiver tightened. "Are you telling me Avery never came in at all yesterday?"

"Never came in and never called to say why. That's just plain inconsiderate, if you ask me. If he had any concern for anyone beside himself —"

Kate broke in and cut off the flow of information. "I need to call him and find out what's going on. Could you give me his number, please?"

Millie rattled off the digits so quickly, Kate had to ask her to repeat them. She thanked Millie, then hung up and tried to collect her thoughts. Avery hadn't so much as made an appearance on Friday. Did his absence have something to do with overhearing the things Renee and Old Man Parsons said about him the previous Sunday?

Kate took a series of deep breaths, hoping to calm herself, but her irritation only grew. Whether the overheard comments disturbed him or not, did Avery really expect them to hold tomorrow's worship service with the church in that state?

Snatching up the phone again, she punched in the number Millie gave her and listened to the soft *brrr . . . brrr . . . brrr.*

After fifteen rings, Kate hung up in disgust. She picked up the receiver again, ready to call Paul and . . .

She stopped with her hand in midair. And tell him what? That his project in grace had derailed? What would that accomplish? In his present condition, she could hardly expect him to come down and set things right.

Kate took a slow, deep breath. This, too, was a part of servanthood, she reminded herself. Just not the fun part.

She headed downstairs again, this time making a beeline for the storage room, where the cleaning supplies were kept. It was time to get to work.

She tackled the sanctuary first, picking up the loose papers and straightening the

Bibles and hymnals in the pew racks, then wiping down the pews until their oak surfaces gleamed.

Brandishing a dust mop, she attacked the floor next, bending low to reach under the pews. Kate knew her back would protest the repetitious bending and straightening by morning. Her arthritic knee was already complaining.

She pushed herself upright and moved to the next row. She had just started swirling the mop in a circular motion when she heard a scuffing sound coming from the foyer.

Kate froze in place and listened. She could hear the light tap of footsteps on the foyer floor, followed by the unmistakable sound of the front door opening and the soft *snick* of the latch when it clicked shut.

Avery! He must have shown up, realized Kate had already caught on to his dereliction of duty, and sneaked back out again.

She dashed to the front door, ready to confront the errant custodian. Prepared to give him a piece of her mind, she flung the door open and stared.

The parking lot stood empty, save for her Honda. No sign of Avery, not even his rusty old pickup. There was simply no sign that anyone at all had been there.

A sudden chill ran up her arms. Kate ducked back inside the church and closed the door firmly before turning the lock.

Propelled by a sense of urgency she couldn't explain, she ran to the back door. After making sure the lock was in place, she slumped against the wall and waited for her heart to stop pounding.

Talk about overreacting! Kate tried to laugh it off. She could almost convince herself it had all been the product of an overactive imagination.

Except for the unmistakable sound of the door opening and closing. She hadn't imagined that.

Kate reminded herself that both doors were locked and she was perfectly safe inside the church, then she collected her cleaning supplies and went down to the basement.

She tried to shake off her uneasiness while she cleared away the Mother's Day Out debris and scraped the glue off the tables.

Who could have been there, and why? More important, why didn't he — or she — make his presence known to her? *It isn't as if I wasn't making plenty of noise,* she mused as she gave the tables a final wipe with a damp rag.

By the time everything was in order, Kate

knew her muscles were going to scream their displeasure at her the following day. She brushed a few stray bits of paper off her slacks and smoothed her hair into place in the ladies' room mirror. It wouldn't do to run into the dry cleaner's and Mercantile looking like the wreck of the *Hesperus.*

She checked her watch and groaned. Too late to run into town at all. It was already time to go back home and fix Paul's lunch. After skipping breakfast that morning and supper the night before, he would surely be ravenous.

She closed the front door behind her, checked to make sure the lock engaged, and headed back to her Honda.

This was hardly the way she had intended to spend her morning.

Chapter Fourteen

She told Paul about her wasted morning while she sliced strips of chicken breast for their chef salad.

"You can't imagine what the downstairs looked like. It obviously hasn't been touched since last Sunday."

Kate arranged portions of the salad on their plates and carried them to the table, along with steaming mugs of coffee.

"All the craft materials the kids used for Mother's Day Out were still lying all over the place. I thought I never was going to get the glue peeled off those tables." She slumped into her chair with a weary sigh.

Instead of commiserating, Paul furrowed his brow. "I wonder what happened to Avery."

Kate's lips tightened. "That's a good question."

After Paul said grace, she picked up her fork and toyed with a piece of lettuce. "I hate to say it, but maybe the naysayers are right. Maybe Avery can't be trusted."

"Did you try to call him?"

"Of course I did." She paused, hearing the sharpness in her tone. "There wasn't any answer. That's when I decided I'd better get busy, or the cleaning wouldn't get done at all."

Paul ate in silence for several minutes. Then he wiped his mouth with his napkin and laid it beside his plate.

"I don't believe it. Everything I've seen in Avery so far points to a man who knows he's hit bottom and has a sincere desire to get his life back on track. I don't intend to give up on him unless I have a rock-solid reason to do so."

Picking up his crutches, he hobbled to the kitchen counter and reached for the phone. "Let me try his number again."

Kate finished the last few bites of her salad while Paul stood with the receiver pressed against his ear. Finally he put the phone back in its cradle and stared out the kitchen window at the towering maple in their tiny backyard.

Kate gathered up the plates and carried them to the sink, trying to decide the best way to reorganize her interrupted day.

She couldn't put off going to the pharmacy. Or the Mercantile, for that matter. The cupboard was almost bare. And she would have to pick up Paul's suit at the cleaner's.

Kate sighed. It looked like her time in the studio that afternoon would be reduced to almost nothing.

She stacked the dishes in the sink, added a squirt of dishwashing liquid, and filled the sink with hot water. Maybe if she hurried, she could redeem enough time to give her at least an hour or two in the studio that evening.

Paul cleared his throat and turned away from the window. "Would you mind driving out to Avery's house to check on him?"

Kate's eyes widened. "Doesn't he live way out north on Sweetwater Street?" In the opposite direction from every place she needed to go.

Paul nodded eagerly. "That's why I'm concerned. He doesn't have any close neighbors to help if he's in any kind of trouble. He might have fallen and hurt himself. It happens to the best of us." He gave her one of his lop-sided grins.

Kate swallowed hard. *Content in all circumstances.* She must try to remember that.

She picked up a dishcloth and began to wash the plates. She looked over her shoulder at Paul and smiled. "Sure, I'd be glad to."

"Why don't you take someone with you, since it is quite a drive? Livvy, maybe?"

"No, she's working today. But LuAnne is at loose ends right now. I'll ask her if she'd like to go." There went the last possibility of any time in her studio that evening. She just hoped her ideas didn't get away from her.

When she had finished washing the dishes, Kate gave the counters and the kitchen table a wipe with a damp dishcloth, then she headed to the phone to call LuAnne.

"It was a good thing you phoned." LuAnne readjusted her seat belt and leaned back in the passenger seat of Kate's Honda. "I'm about to go stir-crazy not having anything to do all day."

She pointed ahead to a small house set back off the road in a cluster of trees. "That's it."

Kate tapped on the brake and turned the Honda into Avery's driveway. The weathered wood siding on the house must have been white at one time. Random chips of paint still clung to the rough boards.

She nodded toward Avery's battered pickup sitting nearby. "At least he's home."

"Watch those steps," LuAnne told her as

they started toward the front porch. "That bottom one looks like it's about ready to fall off."

"It still is." Kate shifted her weight just in time to keep from falling. "Be careful. The top one isn't much better."

Maybe Paul was right, and Avery had injured himself. There seemed to be a multitude of danger spots just waiting for an accident to happen. She extended her hand to LuAnne and helped her up onto the porch.

LuAnne clung to Kate's arm until she regained her balance, then chuckled at the expression on Kate's face. "Doesn't look like much, does it?"

She took a moment to pat her red hair into place and straighten the jeweled necklace eyeglasses holder that hung around her neck.

"This place has been in Avery's family for generations. It was paid off long ago, which is the only reason Avery has a place to live. As spotty as his work record is, he'd never be able to make the payments on a place of his own."

Kate eyed the screen door hanging from one hinge. Would the whole thing fall on top of her when she knocked?

To her relief, it stayed put, although it

rattled in its frame like a pair of castanets the moment she applied her knuckles to it.

Kate looked at LuAnne. "As loose as the door is, that probably didn't make much of a sound inside the house. Do you think he could hear it?"

"I doubt it. Here, let me take a crack at it." LuAnne yanked the screen open and pounded on the front door with her fist.

Kate stared at her surroundings while they waited for an answer, looking out across what once must have been a grassy lawn, now a tangled expanse of weeds. Across the driveway, a small shed was in imminent danger of being swallowed up by kudzu vines.

A couple of minutes passed without an answer. "It doesn't make sense," Kate said, concern outweighing her irritation at having her day disrupted. "If his truck is here, surely he's home."

LuAnne hammered at the front door again. "Avery? You in there?"

They both pressed their ears to the door and listened intently.

LuAnne shot a look at Kate. "Did you hear that? Sounded like a moan to me."

Kate nodded and rattled the knob. "Avery, it's Kate Hanlon and LuAnne Matthews. Can you hear us? Are you all right?"

A faint voice responded. "Hold on, I'm comin' as fast as I can."

Moments later the door swung open. Avery Griffin propped himself against the frame, blinking in the sunlight. His hair stood up in all directions, and a gray pallor tinged his features.

"Goodness," LuAnne burst out, "you look like death warmed over!"

"That's pretty much the way I feel too." Avery scraped a calloused hand across his stubbly chin. The rasping sound reminded Kate of sandpaper.

"Pardon my manners, but I've got to go sit back down." He staggered across the room and flopped onto the couch, waving at them to come inside.

LuAnne took a seat in an overstuffed chair covered with faded orange and yellow flowers. Kate perched on the edge of its mate and tried to find her voice.

"Are you all right, Avery? Paul asked us to come out here. He's concerned about you."

"You drove all the way out here because you were worried about me?"

A gentle smile creased Avery's cheeks, giving him an almost angelic appearance. "Someone kept calling earlier. Was that him?"

Kate nodded. "He knew you hadn't been

by the church, and he wanted to make sure nothing was wrong."

"Tell him I apologize for not answering and for makin' you drive out all this way. I just wasn't able to get to the phone. I've been sick as a dog the last couple of days."

Kate leaned forward. "Is there anything we can do for you? Do you need to see a doctor?"

"I think it's pretty much run its course by now." Avery pressed his hand against his stomach and grimaced.

"I stopped by the church Thursday afternoon. Pastor Paul has shown a lot of faith in me, and I didn't want to let him down. I thought I'd get an early start on the cleaning instead of waiting until Friday.

"The place was a mess, but there was still a raft of kids there. Cute little things, and they looked like they were havin' a great time. I didn't want to try to work with them around, so I figured I'd wait and come in early Friday morning.

"On my way out, I stopped in the kitchen. I was feeling a little peckish, so I thought I'd check the refrigerator and see if there was anything to snack on."

He shook his head. "The only thing in there was a plate of deviled eggs."

"Eggs?" LuAnne's lips rounded into an *O*,

and her eyebrows shot straight up.

"Uh-huh. My mama used to make the best deviled eggs in the county. I never could resist 'em." Avery gave a weak chuckle, then his face twisted. When the spasm had passed, he went on.

"I shoulda resisted these, though. They must have had something in them that didn't agree with me. They just about did me in."

Kate couldn't help exchanging a quick glance with LuAnne.

Avery shuddered, then looked up at Kate. "Tell Pastor Paul I'll try to get in this evening and get the cleaning done. You can't hold church with the place in a mess like that."

"No, don't worry about that. It's all been taken care of. I'm just sorry to hear you've been so sick."

She got to her feet, and LuAnne followed her lead. "Is there anything we can do for you before we leave?" Kate asked. "Do you need anything from the store?"

Avery shook his head. "I haven't been able to keep much down except crackers and soda, and I have plenty of those on hand."

He started to rise, then sank back onto the couch. "I'd see you to the door, ladies, but I just don't think my legs will hold me up. Would you please tell Pastor Paul I'm sorry I let him down this week?"

"I'll do that," Kate promised, her conscience smarting like mad.

"Tell him I ought to be back on my feet in a day or two, and he can count on me to have the church clean as a whistle next Friday."

"I'll tell him."

"And bless you both for comin' out to check on me." The gratitude in his voice made Kate feel even guiltier for her earlier doubts.

"You just take care of yourself, darlin'," LuAnne told him. "And call if you need anything, you hear?"

Kate didn't risk another glance at LuAnne until she had made the turn back onto Sweetwater and was heading back to town. Sure enough, LuAnne's expression held the same sense of horror Kate felt.

LuAnne finally broke the silence. "You know as well as I do where those eggs came from, don't you?"

Kate nodded. "I noticed the cut-glass plate when I set my chicken enchiladas down next to them. No one else brought deviled eggs to the potluck."

LuAnne groaned. "So they sat out on the

table all morning, and who knows how long it was until someone put them back in the refrigerator."

"You're right. It could have been hours later, or even Sunday night. And they were sitting in the fridge until Avery found them on Thursday." Kate shuddered. "It's a good thing it only made him sick."

"You're not kidding. We could have been plannin' his funeral instead." LuAnne slid a sidelong glance at Kate. "So are you going to tell Renee?"

Kate could hear the chuckle in her voice. "No, I don't think so. It wouldn't make things any better for Avery, and Renee would be mortified to know there were that many eggs left over from the potluck in the first place."

LuAnne burst out laughing. "You're probably right."

Just ahead, a slender form darted across the road and disappeared into the trees on the other side. Startled, Kate hit her brakes. The car squealed to a halt.

Kate waited until she could coax her fingers loose from the steering wheel. "Sorry for the sudden stop. Are you all right?"

"I'll be fine," LuAnne assured her. "Did you see who it was?"

Kate had no trouble recognizing the worn

bomber jacket. "I saw him, but I don't know his name. Do you know who he is?"

"He looked a little familiar, but I can't place him. And I know just about everybody in town."

LuAnne twisted around to peer out the side window at the spot where the boy had faded into the line of trees. "Where's he going in such a hurry, anyway? There's nothin' special back in those woods." A puzzled frown puckered her forehead.

"Don't worry about it." Kate took a deep breath and set the car in motion again. "It's just that I've seen him a couple of times before. I ran into him the other day . . . literally."

She filled LuAnne in on their collision on the sidewalk. "It's really no big deal. I was just curious."

LuAnne leaned back in her seat. "Now it's going to bother me until I figure it out. He reminds me of someone, but I can't think who it is."

Kate switched to what she hoped would be a happier topic. "So what are Loretta's plans for the diner?" Her heart sank when she saw the look that shadowed LuAnne's face.

"Your guess is as good as mine. She's keepin' everyone in the dark, including me.

She tells me she hasn't made up her mind what to do yet. Says she just might take the insurance settlement and retire. And then there's that new outfit that wants to buy the place."

"The French restaurant Bernie was talking about?"

LuAnne nodded, and Kate slowed to yield to a truck merging in from Pine Ridge Road. "She isn't serious, is she? Close down the Country Diner?"

"I don't know what's goin' on in the woman's mind these days." LuAnne's voice thickened. "That place is her life — and mine too — but now she's talking about how she'd like to start taking things easier instead of bein' on her feet in that kitchen all day."

"I can understand that," Kate said slowly. "But it's hard to think of life in Copper Mill without the Country Diner. It must be even worse for the people who've been here far longer than Paul and I have."

LuAnne pulled a tissue out of her sleeve and blew her nose. "What's she going to do all day? That's what I'd like to know. My feet get tired too, but I'd rather go home and soak them every night than miss out on the chance to see all my friends and catch up on what's goin' on around town. At least

J.B. has another job to go to if this one disappears."

She dabbed at her nose again, then crumpled the tissue in her hand. "I've got to do something, though. My little bit of savings won't last forever, and the bills just keep pilin' up. Much as I hate to admit it, I've put in a few applications around town, even some in Pine Ridge. I haven't heard back on any of them, though."

Kate gripped the steering wheel tighter and tried to mask her surprise. "Do you think you're jumping the gun? Loretta might decide to reopen after all, or maybe if she sells, you could get a job at the new restaurant and at least keep working in the same place."

LuAnne's face twisted. "I thought about that, but honestly, Kate, can you see me wearin' some frilly uniform and trying to fit in a ritzy place like that?"

Instead of answering, Kate merely asked, "Does she know how you feel?"

"Darlin', have you ever known me to hide my feelin's? Let's just say she knows exactly where I stand and leave it at that. She'd be hurting the whole community, not just me. The idea of losin' the diner is a terrible thing. Just terrible."

But did Loretta know the rest of the town

shared LuAnne's feelings? And would it have any bearing on her decision if she did?

LuAnne's grim voice broke into Kate's thoughts. "Would you mind droppin' me off at the library? I need to check out some books on writin' a résumé."

"No problem. I just wish I could do something to help." Kate put on her blinker and pulled up to the curb on Main Street.

LuAnne took another swipe at her nose with the tissue. She started to open the door, then pointed at the newspaper office across the street from the library. "Have you seen this week's *Chronicle*?"

"Not yet." Kate hedged. In truth, she hadn't given the paper more than a passing glance since the article about the crash.

"Take a look at the ad on page seven when you get a chance."

"What ad? What are you talking about?"

"I'm not going to say another word. Just read it. That'll tell you all you need to know about what folks think about the prospect of the diner closin' down for good."

LuAnne stepped out on the curb. "Thanks for takin' me along. I needed to feel like I had some purpose in life again."

She closed the door, then swung it open again and leaned back inside the car. "And thanks for lettin' me spout off about Loretta and whatever she's plannin' to do with the diner."

"No problem." Kate checked her watch against the town clock tower, hoping it was running fast. She wrinkled her nose when the two showed the same time right down to the minute.

Some of the local businesses kept shorter hours on Saturdays. She would have to hurry if she wanted to make it to the dry cleaner's and the pharmacy before they closed.

She would barely have enough time to do her grocery shopping at the Mercantile and get home to make supper. Servanthood was more time consuming than she'd expected.

But one thing she knew. If she didn't accomplish one other thing that afternoon, she was going to stop at the church on her way home and make sure there weren't any more of those toxic eggs left!

Chapter Fifteen

"Are you sure you're up to doing this?"

"I'm fine, honey." Paul finished putting a Windsor knot in his tie and gave her a reassuring smile. "Eli is here in case anything goes wrong. Just be sure to bring my Bible, and we'll be on our way."

Kate watched him make his way out to the living room. He had tried so hard to look normal for his first public appearance since his accident.

The jacket of the charcoal pinstripe suit she picked up at the cleaner's the day before hung perfectly on his athletic shoulders. From the waist up, he looked handsome and fit.

The tailored effect was marred somewhat by the dark gray sweatpants he'd changed into after finding there was no way the matching charcoal slacks would fit over his moon boot.

She heard him giving Eli the same kind of

assurances she had heard since bringing him home from the hospital. "It probably wasn't necessary to drag you out early, but I appreciate having you here, just in case."

Kate followed the men out into the living room, trying not to laugh. The man needed help getting into his clothes, for goodness' sake.

He did admit to needing Eli's help getting down the step into the garage where Kate's Honda was parked, but he insisted he was fine, perfectly ready to preach a sermon.

Eli showed a knack for rendering aid without making his assistance obvious to Paul. Once he had made sure Paul was situated comfortably in the passenger seat, Eli got into the rear and held the crutches across his lap.

"I might as well leave my truck here and ride over and back with you. No sense using two vehicles when one will do."

Kate gathered up their Bibles and locked the door behind her, making a mental note to bake a special batch of chocolate-chip cookies in return for Eli's tactful help.

"Good. Nobody else is here yet."

Kate noted the relief in Paul's voice when they pulled into the church parking lot. He had insisted on leaving early so they would arrive ahead of the rest of the congregation.

He might insist he was doing fine, but his masculine pride obviously wasn't ready for a crowd of observers in the event his performance on crutches wasn't quite as graceful as he hoped.

Kate went on ahead to open the front door, leaving the two men to work out the logistics of Paul's exit from the car. Better to preserve his dignity than hover over him like an anxious mother hen.

He *was* fine, she reminded herself. Paul was right: his injury could have been far worse. She thought back to the long evening spent in the emergency room and wondered how Eppie Barlow's husband was getting along.

Thanks to Eli, Paul made it from the car into the church without any mishaps and had settled himself in a chair on the platform by the time the first worshippers arrived. Their show of concern for him warmed Kate, although she noted a good number of them refrained from venturing across the aisle to greet her as well.

She lifted her chin, determined not to show how the pointed omission stung. Someday soon the truth would be known, and she could put this painful chapter in her life behind her.

After the opening hymn, Paul made his way to the pulpit, navigating with his crutches like an expert. When he set them aside and steadied himself with his hands on either side of the pulpit, the congregation burst into applause.

Kate's eyes misted over, and from the roughness in Paul's voice when he began the opening prayer, she knew he felt as deeply touched as she did.

Help him get through the service, Lord. Give him the strength he needs, and the wisdom to know when he's overdoing it. And help me quit worrying so I can focus on worshipping you.

The rest of the service went smoothly. Kate knew she could relax when she heard Sam Gorman play the final notes of the closing hymn. As he segued into the postlude, she gathered up her coat and purse.

Livvy circled around the knot of people who crowded the platform to speak to Paul and headed straight for Kate.

"I'm so sorry. I would have been over to help out yesterday, but I had to make up for the time I took off work when I was sick last week."

She clasped Kate's hands. "I feel like a

bad friend."

Kate pulled her hands free so she could wrap her arms around Livvy and give her a warm hug. "You'd have to do a lot worse than that to call yourself a bad friend, Livvy Jenner."

Livvy glanced over her shoulder and lowered her voice. "Any more ideas on the Mustang caper? Or have you had any time to think about it with all that's been going on?"

"I've hardly had a moment to call my own since I got the news about Paul being hurt." Kate peered between the well-wishers to check on him.

"I remember when Justin broke his arm playing football." Livvy patted her on the shoulder. "It's a full-time job, isn't it?"

"And then some." Kate forced a laugh. She hesitated before continuing but knew Livvy wouldn't make light of her feelings.

"To be honest, I'm frustrated. And that makes me feel incredibly guilty, but it's hard for me to adjust when my regular routine is thrown for a loop like this.

"On top of all the usual things, there's taking care of Paul, plus trying to solve the Mustang caper" — she grinned at Livvy's term for the diner mystery — "plus needing to work on that special order. I did tell you about that, didn't I?"

At Livvy's look of surprise, she quickly brought her friend up to date.

Livvy's eyes shone. "That's wonderful, Kate! I'm so pleased for you. It's time your work started getting the recognition it deserves."

Kate felt her cheeks grow warm from Livvy's praise. "Thanks. I have to admit it was a morale boost to get that order just when everything else in my life seems to be going crazy."

She checked again to see how Paul was getting along. He had returned to his seat in the chair, but he still looked like his energy level was high.

Livvy wore her practical-librarian look. "There has to be a way to manage things so you can get it all done. What's on for tomorrow? More on the car mystery?"

"I'm afraid that's going to have to go on the back burner for the moment. I really ought to get to work on that fanlight. No, make that I really *need* to. I've got to focus on it before the time gets away from me."

She shot another look toward the platform. Paul's smile looked a bit strained. Maybe the pain medication was wearing off.

"I'd better get Paul home now, Livvy. Thanks for the sympathy. It'll all work out somehow."

Livvy gave Kate's arm an affectionate squeeze. "Of course it will. What you need is to get some time in your studio and lose yourself in the creative process. Just step back from all the other stuff for a bit. You'll be able to look at things from a clearer perspective."

Kate saw Eli moving forward to help Paul retrieve his crutches. Apparently he had the same idea she did.

"Thanks, Livvy. You always make me feel better. God really blessed me by giving me a friend like you."

Kate slipped out of the church to retrieve her car and pull it around to the front entrance, then she waited for Eli to help Paul get settled in the passenger seat. The two men talked basketball on the drive home, leaving her free to mull over her conversation with Livvy.

I really do need to relax more and not get stressed over things I can't change.

She glanced over, noting that Paul looked tired but still wore a smile. *He's taking all this much better than I am. As he keeps reminding me, it's only a broken ankle.*

She pulled into the garage, determined to get her mind off the things that were weighing her down and focus on counting her blessings instead.

For one thing, Paul wasn't totally incapacitated; he was up and around, even if he was moving more slowly than usual.

For another, he had a wonderful attitude. Some men would be griping and complaining from sunup to sunset.

They also had a great friend in Eli, who stood ready to help out any way he could. She stepped out of the Honda and watched him help Paul out of the car.

And then there was Livvy. God truly had bestowed a special blessing with their friendship.

Kate bumped the driver's door shut with her hip and let herself into the house with a lighter heart, leaving Paul in Eli's capable hands.

She set the Bibles on the arm of the couch and stepped into the kitchen while Paul and Eli followed more slowly.

"Thanks for your help," Paul said to Eli. "I appreciate being able to call on you."

The younger man patted him on the shoulder. "I'm glad everything went smoothly. Let me know if there's anything else I can do. Right now, it looks like you're ready for a nap."

"How about having lunch first?" Kate asked. "You don't need to be skipping any more meals, Paul. Eli, would you like to stay and eat with us?"

Eli's eyes lit up. "I wouldn't want to impose."

"I'd say we're the ones who imposed on you," Paul told him. "Why don't you let us turn the tables and do something for you in return?"

"We're having pot roast." Kate opened the oven to check its progress, releasing a tantalizing aroma into the air. "I had it on time bake. It should be ready in about twenty minutes. I'm fixing potatoes and gravy too," she added.

Eli closed his eyes and sniffed appreciatively. "I'll stay. You don't have to twist my arm one bit more. Your cooking isn't something I would ever turn down without a good reason."

Kate bustled around the kitchen finishing the last-minute preparations while the men retired to the living room and continued their conversation.

She set three places at the table then pulled the roast from the oven and poured the drippings into a pan. She added flour, milk, and a dash of salt, stirring the mixture carefully to keep any lumps from forming.

The men's voices formed a pleasant hum in the background. Kate transferred the thickened sauce to a gravy boat and pulled her favorite platter from the cupboard.

Taking out a sharp knife, she began slicing the pot roast, only half listening while the topic of conversation moved from basketball to the previous month's Chamber of Commerce meeting to the latest news around town.

But Eli's next comment caught her full attention.

"I hear the fellow who owns the Mustang that hit the diner got a pleasant surprise in yesterday's mail. His insurance company sent him a settlement check, and it sounds like he came out quite well on the deal."

"I don't follow you," Paul said. "Why would that surprise him?"

Kate set the knife down and listened.

"For one thing, the insurance company gave him a hard time at first. Out of all the cars he has cluttering up his property, it seems the Mustang was the only one he had insured besides that '56 Chevy he drives."

"I've seen that Chevy. He did a nice job on the restoration."

"The insurance company also had a problem with him not reporting the Mustang as stolen right away. But since Sheriff Roberts wrote it up as a theft, and the car was totaled, they didn't have much choice but to cover the loss. And from what I hear around town, they shelled out a pretty fair amount for it."

"That seems odd," Paul said. "Why have full coverage on a car he didn't drive?"

Kate peered through the doorway and saw Eli shrug. "That's a good question. Myers is kind of a character, though. There's no telling what makes him do some of the things he does."

Paul chuckled. "I suspect the same thing could be said for a good many of us."

Kate heard Eli laugh as she returned to arrange the roast on the platter and carry the serving dishes to the table. Then he cleared his throat, and his voice took on a more solemn tone.

"As tired as you must be today, Paul, it probably isn't a good time to bring this up. But I'm not sure there ever will be a good time."

"You know you can talk to me anytime, Eli. You're my friend as well as a church member, and I'm always glad to hear from you, whether it's good news or not."

What now? Kate set the gravy boat next to the bowl of potatoes and strained to listen.

"Thanks, I appreciate that. I've been sitting on this for a few days, trying to decide what to do, or whether I needed to do anything. I still haven't made up my mind yet, but I think it's something you should be aware of at any rate."

"Go on." Paul's tone carried the same curiosity Kate felt.

"I stopped by the church the other day to pick up some tools I'd left in the storage shed, and I noticed the lawn mower was missing."

"That's odd. Did you ask Avery about it?"

"I would have, but he wasn't around that morning. I caught Millie just as she was leaving her office, and she told me she'd seen Avery loading it onto his truck and driving away with it."

"I'm surprised she didn't say anything to me about it. Do you think the mower needed some repair?"

"That's just it," Eli said. "I checked it over before we put it away last fall. It was running fine then."

"Well, whatever his reason for taking it, maybe he's brought it back by now."

Kate stepped to the door to call the men to the table and saw Eli's pained look.

"I went by yesterday and checked. It's still missing, Paul. I don't know what's going on, but I thought you should know, especially in light of the comments some of the church members are making about Avery."

Paul noticed Kate and clapped Eli on the shoulder. "It looks like it's time to eat. Thanks for telling me. I'm sure everything is fine, but it's good to be aware of what's going on."

Kate rinsed out the sink and squeezed the water out of the dishrag. After one last glance around the kitchen to make sure she hadn't missed any dirty dishes, she wandered into the living room and stretched out on the couch.

She settled her head into the cushion with a grateful sigh. Despite her misgivings about Paul returning to the pulpit so soon after being injured, the day had gone without mishap.

Once Eli left, Paul headed to the bedroom for his much-needed nap, leaving her with an afternoon to herself.

Kate stirred on the couch. She ought to take advantage of this time, do something to sort out the tangled maze her life had become of late. But she didn't have the least idea what that "something" would be.

Her eyelids drifted shut, and she let herself sink into the soft cushion. Maybe a nap of her own wouldn't be a bad idea.

Livvy was right, she needed time to let the

cares of the world fade away and get back to feeling like herself again. Things would start coming together again the following day. She just knew it.

Chapter Sixteen

Kate closed her Bible and leaned back in her rocking chair, luxuriating in the peace of the early morning hour. The faint creak of the rocker was the only sound intruding on the stillness in the living room.

It was sheer bliss after the chaos of the previous week.

She closed her eyes and reflected on the verse she had just read in James: *Consider it pure joy, my brothers, whenever you face trials of many kinds, because you know that the testing of your faith develops perseverance.*

She couldn't count having to care for Paul as a trial. Far from it! But her recent feelings of being overwhelmed would qualify — no doubt about it.

The golden beams of the sun's first rays slipped in through the cloudy sliding-glass doors. Kate watched them creep across the moss green shag carpet, feeling a fresh surge of optimism.

A new day meant new beginnings, and today she felt more than ready to get into her studio and dive into her new project with abandon.

The distinctive clicking sound of Paul's crutches told her that he was up and about even before he appeared in the doorway to their bedroom.

Kate looked up at him and smiled. They had so much to be grateful for, this "inconvenience" notwithstanding.

Paul lowered himself onto the couch like Old Man Parsons when his rheumatism was acting up. "Could you help me get my foot up here on the cushion? This boot feels like it weighs a ton this morning."

"Of course." Kate lifted his foot, being careful not to jar it when she swung his leg around and set it gently on the couch cushion.

Paul slid a couple of throw pillows behind his back and scrunched them into place. "Perfect."

He closed his eyes, then opened them again. "I meant to bring along a bedroom pillow to prop up my foot. Would you mind getting it for me? And maybe bring an afghan to throw over my lap?"

Kate looked down at him and tilted her head. "Is it just my imagination, or do you think you might have overdone it a bit yesterday?"

"I guess I must have. I didn't think so at the time, but I really feel wiped out this morning. Maybe part of it's due to staying awake thinking about what Eli said."

"You mean about Avery taking the lawn mower?" Kate called as she padded down the hall to the bedroom to get the pillow and afghan. When she returned, she plumped the pillow under his foot, then spread the throw across his legs.

Paul nodded. "I don't want to think badly of him, but I can't think of any reason for him to be driving off with a piece of equipment like that." His lips tightened. "Especially a piece of equipment no one would be likely to miss until spring."

A knot formed in Kate's stomach. "You don't think Renee and Old Man Parsons were right about him stealing from the church, do you?"

"I don't even want to consider that as a possibility, but I honestly don't know. There may be some simple explanation for what he did, but I haven't been able to come up with one yet. And I don't know whether to confront him about it or wait and see what happens."

"You'll know what to do when the time

comes. You always do." Kate leaned over and dropped a light kiss on his forehead. "Now, how about a steaming mug of coffee? Then I'll make you some breakfast."

Paul's eyelids closed. "The coffee sounds good for starters. But just a slice of toast for breakfast. I don't feel like trying anything heavy this morning."

Kate brought him a mug of coffee, then returned to the kitchen to fix him some toast with a thick layer of apple butter spread over it.

"Why don't you just sit still and take it easy? You've been pushing pretty hard for a man who just found out he isn't Superman. You need some downtime."

Paul took the plate from her and gave her a weak grin. "That's the best advice I've heard all day."

Kate aimed a playful swat at his shoulder. "Don't try to win me over with flattery. It's only seven thirty in the morning."

"Still . . ."

Kate laughed and shook her head. "I'm going to get dressed and head for my studio. If you need anything, just sing out."

The doorbell stopped her in her tracks. "Who could that be at this hour? Renee's the only one who shows up this early."

She tightened the belt of her robe and

smoothed her hair before opening the door.

Pete MacKenzie, pastor of Copper Mill Presbyterian Church, smiled at her from the doorstep. "Hi, Kate. I just wanted to stop by and check on Paul."

He glanced down, taking in her attire, then gave her a sheepish grin. "I guess it's still a little early for a visit."

Kate stepped back to let him in. "No, it's fine. Paul is already up, and I'm going to be working in my studio, so I'm sure he'll be glad for the company."

She paused in the entryway. "Would you like some coffee?"

Pete's eyes lit up. "I'd love some."

"Paul's in the living room on the couch. I'll bring it to you in a minute."

Kate returned to the kitchen, filled an oversized mug with the steaming brew, and carried it into the living room. Paul already looked happier for having someone to talk to, she noted.

Good. That would give him something to take his mind off his discomfort. She left the two men talking about how soon they could get to one of Pete's favorite fishing holes and went to the bedroom to dress.

Since she planned to work in her studio all day, she donned a pair of comfortable slacks and a light blue sweatshirt with Texas wildflowers on the front.

She brushed her strawberry-blonde hair and pulled it back from her face with a pair of silver clips. After applying a dash of makeup, she felt ready to start a productive day.

As she passed through the living room, she noticed that Pete had pulled her rocking chair over to the couch, apparently ready to settle in for an extended visit. Kate freshened up both men's coffees and cleared away Paul's breakfast plate, then carried out a tray laden with sugar, cream, and a plate of oatmeal cookies. After wiping down the kitchen counter, she set off for her studio.

When she was halfway down the hall, the doorbell caught her in midstride. She retraced her steps to the entryway and opened the door.

"Good morning, Kate. Is this too early to stop by?"

"Not at all." Kate smiled up at Lucas Gregory, the rector of St. Lucy's Episcopal Church. "In fact, Pete MacKenzie beat you to it."

She waved him toward the living room and went to fetch another mug. She poured the last of the coffee into it and started a new pot.

Returning to the living room, Kate handed

the mug to Lucas, who thanked her with a smile.

"Would you mind bringing me a pill and a glass of water, hon?" Paul used both hands to shift his right leg higher on the pillow. "The pain's starting to kick in with a vengeance."

She brought him the medication and water and noticed the lines etched around the corners of his eyes. "What else can I do for you?"

"Maybe fluff up that pillow a bit?"

Kate slipped the cushion from under his foot and shook new life into it before tucking it back in place. "Is that better?"

Paul settled back and gave a contented sigh. "You're a good woman. Have I told you that lately?"

"A true Proverbs 31 woman," Pete quipped. "Could I trouble you for a little more of that coffee, Kate?"

"Sure." She reached for the mug he held out to her. "I have a fresh batch brewing. It should be ready in a few minutes."

On her way back to the kitchen, the doorbell buzzed again. Kate made a detour to the front door.

Bobby Evans stepped inside and grinned. "I hear we've moved our coffee hour over here today."

"Maybe we should move it here permanently," Lucas called. "I like the coffee here a whole lot better than the diner's."

Kate laughed. "Don't let LuAnne or Loretta hear you say that." She fixed a mug of coffee for Bobby and brought the pot with her to pour a fresh round for the rest.

She was beginning to wonder whether she'd ever get to her studio that morning.

"So, how did your day go?" Livvy asked when she called that evening. "Did you get a lot done on your new project?"

Kate sagged against the kitchen counter and readjusted the receiver against her ear.

"Would you believe I never even set foot in the studio? Between taking care of Paul and answering the door for his visitors, I've been on the run all day long."

"That's a shame. Maybe tomorrow will be better. Wow, listen to that wind! Is it blowing as hard at your place as it is at ours? Sounds like we have a major storm building up."

Kate glanced toward the kitchen window. Dark clouds blotted out the moon. Even in the faint light, she could see the maple branches swaying wildly.

"And just when I was thinking happy thoughts about spring being right around the corner."

"Dream on. There are no guarantees around here this time of year. You're not in San Antonio anymore."

"That's the truth." Kate shifted the receiver to her other hand. "Did I tell you Millie stopped by?"

"With a list of phone calls Paul could make while he's just lounging around, no doubt." Laughter bubbled in Livvy's voice.

"Close. She brought by a rough draft of next week's bulletin for him to approve, along with a stack of church mail that came in this morning. She told him she assumed he would be able to stay current with his correspondence, even if he can't do much walking at the moment."

Livvy made a *tsk-tsk* sound.

Kate ticked off the other items on her fingers. "She also said it would be helpful to her if he could plan out his sermon texts at least a month in advance, so she created a form for him to fill out."

"Oh, my goodness. She's really on a micromanagement roll, isn't she?"

"That's not all. Then she pulled out that calendar she keeps on her desk and went over everything on it with him. She wanted to know when he thought he'd be up to working in the church office again so she would know which appointments needed to be rescheduled."

She looked over her shoulder toward the kitchen doorway and lowered her voice. "I don't think it made her very happy when he said he wasn't sure when he would be back. He really did more yesterday than he should have, and he's paying for it now."

Livvy's sigh drifted through the receiver. "Men! They always think they're invincible."

"Well, this one just had a reality check. It's a good thing he works hard at staying in shape. The doctor told him that should make the healing process go more smoothly."

"Let's hope so. It sounds like you both had quite a day. I'll hang up now and let you get some rest."

"Thanks for calling. It really helped."

"No problem. That's what friends are for. Be sure to bundle up tonight, maybe get out an extra blanket or two. It looks like it's going to be a cold night."

Kate said good night, then set the phone back on the kitchen counter, wishing she were already curled up in bed.

She pushed herself to straighten up the living room and kitchen before shutting down for the night. By the time she crawled into bed, Paul was already asleep.

Kate lay beside him in the darkness, listening to the soft rattle of sleet against the window. Careful not to jostle Paul, she snuggled closer to him and let her muscles relax, feeling extremely weary and ready for sleep to claim her.

Instead, scenes from the long day played through her mind like a Powerpoint presentation:

Millie Lovelace pointing to her calendar.

Father Lucas and Pastors Pete and Bobby drinking endless mugs of her fresh-ground coffee.

She rolled onto her other side and pulled the blanket up to her chin. Why did her mind keep dwelling on Paul's visitors, like a pesky fly that refused to go away?

She went back over them, one by one, trying to remember if any of them had said something that might have some bearing on the mystery she was trying to solve.

Like a flash of lightning, the answer suddenly blazed into Kate's mind.

She had it all wrong. It didn't have anything to do with that day's visits. It was Eli's comment the previous day about Roland Myers coming into a sizable payment from the insurance settlement he received on the Mustang.

But she had seen the elderly man outside

the bank on Friday, complaining to his friend about being turned down for a loan because he was a poor credit risk.

Why would he have been trying to get a loan when he had already received a substantial check from his insurance company?

No, wait. Eli said that Myers had gotten the check in the mail on Saturday. What if . . .

Kate's eyes flew open. What if Roland Myers wasn't running a chop shop after all? What if he had schemed to defraud his insurance company instead?

She sat up in bed, careful not to wake Paul, and wrapped her arms around her knees.

Roland Myers needed money. That was obvious from the conversation she overheard on Friday afternoon. If he had set up a plan to make a fraudulent claim on the Mustang and the plan apparently failed, that would explain his application for credit at the bank as well as his pique when the bank turned him down.

Eli said Myers had been pleasantly surprised when he got the insurance check on Saturday.

I'll just bet he was.

Kate went over her new theory, examining it from every side without finding a flaw. It made more sense than anything else that had come to light so far. Definitely an angle that needed further investigation.

She lay back down, closed her eyes, and nestled into her pillow. One thing was clear: when things settled down just a bit, she needed to pay Roland Myers another visit.

CHAPTER SEVENTEEN

Livvy's prediction of a winter storm was borne out when Kate awakened the next morning to a world coated with ice. She looked out on the sparkling scene and pressed her finger against the delicate tracery of frost etched on the bedroom window.

"Paul, you're not going to believe this!"

"What is it? What's wrong?" He emerged from the bathroom, leaning on his crutches, and clicked his way across the room.

"We had quite a storm last night. Look at what it's done." She pushed the curtain back farther so he could see. "It's beautiful. Beautiful and terrible, all at once."

Paul joined her at the window and slipped an arm around her waist. He pursed his lips and let out a low whistle. "We sure never got anything like this in San Antonio."

Kate rested her head on his shoulder. "That's what Livvy said last night. I heard the sleet starting just before I went to sleep, but I never expected anything like this."

The arctic blast had turned Smoky Mountain Road into a glittering fairyland. Everything, from power lines to fence rails to tree limbs, looked as if it had been encased in a sheet of glass.

Kate shook her head. "It's going to be a while before there's any traffic. Just look at that layer of ice on the road."

"I wouldn't try it, even with chains. I hope you weren't planning on going anywhere." Paul pointed across the pavement where a tangle of broken limbs jutted into the road. "There's probably damage like that all over town. I hope somebody comes to move those pretty soon. That's a real traffic hazard."

He leaned forward to survey their front yard. "It looks like everything here is okay, at least."

Kate started. "I got so caught up in the beauty of it all, I forgot to think about any damage. I suppose I ought to check the rest of the place."

She hurried from room to room, peering out each window in turn.

"Everything looks all right," she called from her studio. Then she went into the living room to peer out the clouded sliding-glass doors. “Oh no.”

Paul joined her, hobbling as quickly as he could. “How bad is it?”

“It’s the maple out back. Come and see.” Kate gestured toward the tree that dominated their postage-stamp-size backyard.

Like the trees across the road, every limb was weighted down by a cocoon of ice. At least half a dozen of them, each thicker than Paul’s arm, had sheered off and lay in a heap around the base of the trunk.

Looking up, she could see where at least a dozen more limbs had snapped loose and were dangling precariously overhead.

Paul’s lips tightened. “That isn’t safe. Those need to be taken off and cleared away.”

Kate touched the frigid glass with her fingertips. “I don’t dare try to tackle it while it’s so slick outside, but once the ice thaws —”

“You aren’t to even think about attempting that on your own. If this had happened last week, I wouldn’t have had any trouble taking care of it myself. But as things are now . . .”

He glared down at his injured leg. “It’s bad enough for one of us to be laid up. We don’t need to risk injury to us both.”

His voice took on a softer, teasing tone.

"Besides, if we're both wearing casts, who's going to run all my errands for me?"

Kate hugged him. "Speaking of taking care of you, why don't we have some coffee, and I'll whip up a couple of omelets."

Thirty minutes later, she carried plates bearing fluffy western omelets to the table. Paul sat in his usual spot, leafing through the previous week's *Chronicle.*

"Have you seen this ad on page seven?" He folded the paper open to that page and handed it to Kate in exchange for his breakfast.

"Page seven? No, but LuAnne mentioned something about it the other day." She looked at the open paper and felt her jaw drop.

The upper half of the page was taken up by a large display ad with a bold headline blazoned across the top: BRING BACK THE COUNTRY DINER!

"Oh my."

Paul lifted a forkful of his omelet. "Wait until you read the rest of it."

Kate scanned the ad quickly, then read aloud:

> "An Open Letter to Loretta Sweet from Your Faithful Customers —
>
> We have heard a rumor that you're

considering retirement instead of reopening our beloved Country Diner. Please, please, please don't do this! Our town would never be the same. We need you, Loretta. Please don't go! Signed . . ."

The rest of the space was taken up by column after column of names. Kate spotted Joe Tucker's, Skip Spencer's and Mayor Lawton Briddle's names among them. At a quick glance, it looked like nearly half the town had added their names to the list.

She lowered the paper and stared at Paul.

He chuckled. "Not exactly subtle, is it?"

"LuAnne told me people were upset, but this . . ." Kate looked at the paper again. "I wonder how Loretta is taking it."

Paul finished the last bite of his omelet before he answered. "I'm surprised we weren't asked to sign it. Frankly, I would have been glad to put my name on it as well. Can you imagine never being able to go in and order another round of biscuits and gravy again?"

He held up his hands when Kate gave him a mock glare. "You're right, much as I share their sentiments, I'll admit this approach is a little heavy-handed. I'd been meaning to go over and see Loretta anyway, before this ad appeared. I guess I'll have to put that on the list of places for my chauffeur to deliver me."

"You're not going anywhere until the ice melts off those roads," Kate told him. "In the meantime, this chauffeur is going to spend some much-needed time in her studio."

She picked up his plate and dropped a kiss on the top of his head. "Call me if you need anything."

Humming, she washed up the dishes and started for her studio. There was one good thing about the storm, she reflected. As dangerous as the roads looked, they shouldn't be interrupted by another spate of unexpected visitors anytime soon.

A loud jangling interrupted her thoughts before she got halfway across the living room. At least the phone was still working.

She hurried back to the kitchen to answer it, breathing a prayer of thanks. It would have been much worse if the phone lines were out too.

To her relief, it was Livvy, calling to see how they were doing and whether they had sustained any storm damage.

"Oh, what a shame," she sympathized after Kate filled her in on the maple's broken limbs. "That's such a beautiful tree! The schools are closed for a snow day, so

Danny and the boys are home. They would come right over to help clear the mess away, but Renee got to them first. There's a big oak limb hanging over her front porch, and her mother is convinced it's going to come crashing into their living room at any moment. You know how persuasive Renee can be when she gets an idea in her head."

Kate smiled. "That may qualify as the understatement of the year."

"The boys are thrilled about playing lumberjack," Livvy went on, "but Danny isn't quite so excited about standing up on a ladder and trying to saw off limbs in freezing weather."

Kate laughed. "I can imagine. Tell Danny not to worry about it. I'm sure he and everybody else will have their hands full trying to clean up their own property. We'll figure out something soon. In the meantime, I'll just stay out of the backyard."

She hung up, wondering how many more times the phone would ring that morning.

As it turned out, that was the only phone interruption of the day. Kate spent the morning in her studio, enjoying the luxury of having an uninterrupted stretch of time to let the possible designs for the fanlight flow from her imagination onto the paper.

The ideas came freely, and Kate was soon

lost in the joy of giving free rein to her creative side. She left her sketching long enough to fix a light lunch for her and Paul and spend time with him, then she returned to the studio.

Several of the designs looked promising, but one in particular stood out.

Kate took a closer look at it and changed a few of the lines. After penciling in the final stroke, she leaned back and scrutinized it detail by detail, checking it from several different angles.

Would it fit the needs of Harry Michaels, her first customer? She thought back to their phone conversation, shortly after Steve had given her the order. Her questions had elicited little information at first, but she pressed on until she learned about Mr. Michaels' passion for gardening. When she mentioned the possibility of a design incorporating some of his favorite flowers, his enthusiasm gave her all the encouragement she needed to make that the focal point of the piece. Would that concept fit the bill?

A slow smile curved her lips, and excitement bubbled up within her.

"Yes," she breathed. "That's the one."

A light tapping broke into her thoughts, and she turned to find Paul framed in the doorway. "Is my favorite artist still in creative mode, or are you ready for a break?"

Kate checked her watch. "Three o'clock! I must have been in my own little world. I had no idea it was getting that late."

She stretched her arms above her head and rolled her neck from side to side. "It was worth it, though. The design I settled on turned out even better than I thought it would."

She held up the sketch for his inspection. "What do you think?"

Paul's face lit up. "It's beautiful! Is that for your special order?"

Kate nodded, delighted at his unreserved approval. She stepped back a few feet and looked at the drawing from a distance, taking in the blend of dogwood and forsythia blossoms.

"Now that I have the design worked out, I can't wait to get started on it." She grinned. "Maybe it's because I've been longing for warmer weather, and those blooms hold out the hope of spring."

Paul moved beside her. "Could you wait long enough to drive me into town? The roads have cleared off, and Loretta has been on my mind all afternoon. I could call her, but I really feel the need to go talk to her."

Kate smirked at him. "So you can plead

your case in person on reopening the diner?"

Paul tapped his forefinger on the tip of her nose. "I'll have you know I'm primarily concerned about her well-being. She's been through a lot lately."

He slanted a playful look at Kate. "Of course, if the diner comes up in the conversation . . ."

"Of course."

Kate fought to keep a straight face but lost the battle and sputtered with laughter. "Give me a few minutes to straighten up here, and then your trusty chauffeur will be back on duty."

"Watch out for ice. You don't need to be taking another spill." Kate braked at the curb in front of Loretta's small yellow house on Barnhill Street.

Paul levered himself out of the Honda's passenger seat without assistance and propped himself up on the edge of the sidewalk.

"It looks like it's all melted off, but I'll be careful. See you in half an hour?"

"That'll be fine," Kate said. "Tell Loretta I'm praying for her."

"I'll do that." Paul swung the car door closed, then proceeded up the flagstone walk to Loretta's front door.

Kate drummed her fingers on the steering wheel, trying to decide what to do with the thirty minutes at her disposal. It wasn't long enough to go home and do anything productive before she needed to be back to pick up Paul.

What about the library? She yearned for a nice long heart-to-heart with Livvy, but half an hour would barely give them a chance to get started. She sighed and shook her head. Better save that for another time.

An idea struck her, and she put the Honda in gear. She could drive around and see how much damage the storm had done here in town.

She drove slowly, circling the Town Green, and noted with relief that the cleanup crews had already been at work, and many of the trees seemed to be intact.

She stopped to let a couple cross Euclid in front of the town hall and did a double take when she spotted Sheriff Roberts' vehicle parked beside the brick building.

Now there was something she could do that wouldn't take all that long. An empty parking spot beckoned just ahead, and Kate pulled into it.

Sheriff Alan Roberts was talking on the

telephone when she opened the door to the sheriff's office. He glanced up and acknowledged her entrance with a brief nod, then pointed toward Skip Spencer and went back to his phone conversation.

Taking the hint, Skip shut the drawer of the filing cabinet and parked on the edge of his desk. "What can we do for you, Missus Hanlon?"

Kate smiled. "I noticed the sheriff's SUV parked outside. I thought I'd check and see if he had any new leads on the Mustang." She looked at Skip hopefully. "Is anything happening on that?"

Skip glanced over his shoulder. When he saw the sheriff still deep in conversation, he turned back to Kate and lowered his voice. "We haven't turned up much of anything yet, but —"

"Skip!" The sheriff hung up the phone and beckoned to his deputy.

Giving Kate an apologetic look, Skip trotted over to the sheriff's desk and drew himself up. "Yes, sir. Is there something you want me to look into?"

"I need last year's report on traffic fines we collected here in town," the sheriff said. "Would you like to look into that for me?"

The deputy's shoulders sagged. His expression reminded her of the way Kisses looked when his food dish was empty.

Poor thing, she mused as Skip returned to the gray metal filing cabinets. He wanted so much to prove to the sheriff that he was capable of being more than a mere paper pusher.

If only he hadn't made so many bloopers in his early days in law enforcement. Everyone made mistakes, of course, but Skip's tended to be more memorable than most.

Kate still chuckled at the thought of Skip arresting Renee Lambert for attempted pickpocketing, when all she was trying to do was adjust Joe Tucker's handkerchief.

The unfortunate incident occurred before she and Paul moved to Copper Mill, but the story had gone down in local legend. Even though she hadn't been around to see it, the mental image of Skip's determination to uphold the law and Renee's subsequent wrath made Kate laugh every time she thought of it.

She took the opportunity to cross the open space to the sheriff's desk. "So have you decided I'm not a criminal mastermind after all?"

The sheriff shook his head. "I never thought that, Kate. I just needed your prints to compare with the others we found at the scene. A lot of our work involves the process of elimination."

His smile softened his craggy face. "Does that help?"

"A little. But I'd feel a lot better if all the loose ends in this case could be tied up." She slipped into the visitor's chair to put herself at eye level with him. "Have you made any progress on finding out who drove that Mustang?"

Sheriff Roberts shook his head again. "At this point, I'm inclined to think it was a transient without any local connections. The prints we took off the steering wheel don't match any of the others we found at the diner . . . or yours or Roland Myers', for that matter. There's nothing to point to it being anyone from around here. More than likely, whoever did it hit the road soon afterward and will never show up around here again."

"So that means . . ."

He shrugged. "There's a possibility, and a strong one, that we may never find out who did it."

Kate's hands clenched in her lap. "That's it? You're giving up?"

"We never give up, but it's probably moving onto a back burner pretty soon. We just don't have anything else to go on."

"Here you are, sir." Skip stepped up

beside them and placed a file folder squarely on the sheriff's desk.

Sheriff Roberts flipped the folder open and handed it back to him after a brief glance. "The mayor asked me for that information. Would you mind running this over to his office for me?"

Skip looked even more crestfallen than before. Maybe being a gofer ranked even lower than a paper pusher.

Sheriff Roberts looked back at Kate. "Anything else?"

She took the hint. "No, that's all I wanted to know. Thank you for your time."

Skip held the door open for her as they passed out into the building's central area. "So did you find out what you needed to?"

"I guess so, but I was really hoping things had moved forward with the Mustang case. It's a shame you don't have any leads to go on."

"No . . ." Skip slowed his pace. "Nothing official, that is."

Kate stopped in her tracks. "What do you mean?"

"I have an idea or two of my own I want to follow up on."

Kate put her hand on his arm. "Like what?"

Skip lowered his voice and spoke out of

the side of his mouth in a way that reminded Kate of a James Cagney movie. "Why would someone take off with that Mustang in the middle of the night? I mean, there were a ton of other cars out there the thief could have taken instead. Someone was after that car specifically."

Kate's pulse fluttered. "Why would he want that car instead of one of the others?"

"There's a big market for parts for classic cars like that. I'd say someone knew exactly what they wanted."

He glanced around and leaned closer to her. "Do you know what a chop shop is?"

Kate bobbed her head up and down, trying to hold back her excitement. "It's a place where stolen cars are dismantled and parted out."

Skip nodded at her as though she were a star pupil. "Exactly. And there's someone around here who used to run one. Any idea who that is?"

So her first instinct had been right all along! Roland Myers had been involved in this all along, not as the victimized owner, but a perpetrator.

"Avery Griffin," Skip punctuated the statement with a knowing nod.

Kate's jaw dropped. "Avery?"

"Yep. He had himself a nice little setup on

the back edge of his property about fifteen years ago. He even served some time in the county jail."

"But . . . but . . ."

"I'm going to be keeping my eye on him," Skip promised. "We'll get a break in the case before long. I can just about guarantee it."

He turned toward the mayor's office, leaving Kate rooted to the floor. Avery, a car thief?

A new thought struck her. Did Paul know?

It was possible. Knowing how strongly he felt about keeping a confidence, she realized that he might have been aware of Avery's checkered past but hadn't told her. If he did know, it was no wonder the news about Avery driving off with the church's lawn mower upset him so much.

Or maybe he would be just as surprised as she to learn about the revelation she had just received. And if that were the case, would it change his mind about keeping Avery on as the church custodian?

She walked out of the building and stood at the top of the concrete steps. Paul would be so disappointed if it turned out that his trust in Avery had been misplaced.

Kate got into her Honda and pulled away from the curb, sick at heart. Much as she wanted to find the person responsible for wrecking the diner, she hoped Paul's intuition hadn't played him false.

"How's Loretta doing?"

Paul set his crutches inside the car and lowered himself onto the passenger seat before he answered.

He turned a bemused look on Kate. "Talkative about some things, tight-lipped about others. I found out, for instance, who the mysterious caller was who reported the crash to the sheriff's office."

Kate caught her breath in a quick gasp. "Who?"

"Elma Swanson. She was coming home late from visiting some friends in Pine Ridge, and saw the hole in the front of the diner when she drove by." He grinned. "She was in such a hurry to get off the phone with the deputy and start calling everyone else she knew that she forgot to leave her name."

Kate laughed. "But what has Loretta decided to do? Did she tell you?"

Paul's grin faded. "I guess I'd have to say Loretta is keeping things to herself about the fate of the diner."

Kate blinked. "She wouldn't even give you a hint?"

Paul shook his head and stared out the

side window. "Not even when I told her how much it would mean to me and the other pastors. She did ask me for a favor, though."

Something in his tone of voice told Kate she'd better brace herself. "And what would that be?"

"She wants me to make an announcement next Sunday from the pulpit. She'd like me to tell the congregation she's tired of getting all the phone calls and having people show up at her door at all hours, and she wants everyone to leave her alone. People from all over town have been pestering her, but she said that would at least let the Faith Briar members know how she feels. She says it's nobody's business but hers whether she reopens, shuts the place down, or sells it to the businessmen who want to open that French restaurant everyone seems to be talking about."

Kate sputtered with laughter. "The poor thing. They must be driving her to distraction if she's ready to go to that length."

"It would seem so." Paul leaned over to massage his injured leg.

"She showed me a log she's been keeping. Seven phone calls yesterday and thirteen the day before. She's only had five so far today, but she tells me it's early yet, and she's sure there'll be more."

"If nothing else, that ought to show her how much people love the diner."

She gave Paul an impish smile. "So what are you going to do about the announcement?"

He groaned. "I haven't decided yet. Maybe I'll ask Millie to include it with the prayer requests when she prints the bulletins this week."

Chapter Eighteen

"Race you to the car."

Kate paused in the act of shrugging into her parka and stared at her husband. "What did you say?"

A cheeky grin split Paul's face. "I said I'd race you to the car." He dropped into a half crouch in the foyer, balancing on his good leg and holding his crutches poised. "Ready?"

Kate reached up to pat his head as she walked past to open the door that led from the foyer to the garage. "Give it a few more weeks, and I might take you up on it. For now, I think just getting to the car is probably enough of an accomplishment."

She pushed the door open wide and swept her arm in a grand gesture. "Your chariot awaits." She let Paul enter the garage ahead of her.

"If I didn't know better, I'd say you were afraid of the challenge."

Kate wrinkled her nose at him, then pushed the button on her remote to open the garage door.

Paul slapped his hand on top of the Honda. "I win."

"What?"

"You didn't tag the car. We were racing, remember? I win."

Kate walked around to the driver's side, slid under the steering wheel, and fixed him with a stern look through the open passenger door. "You are getting entirely too feisty, Reverend Hanlon."

Paul lowered himself inside the car. "Is that a complaint?"

Kate turned the key and let the motor run a moment while she reached across the seat and wrapped her arms around his neck. "No complaints here. I'm just glad you're getting better."

"Not to brag," he went on while she backed the Honda out of the driveway, "but I am a lot more mobile than I was a week ago."

Kate wagged her finger at him. "Enough to get yourself in trouble if you don't behave. Just take it easy and follow the doctor's instructions."

She shifted into Drive and started off down Smoky Mountain Road. "I'm delighted you're feeling so well, but we don't want any setbacks."

What a relief to be able to joke like this instead of fretting about his injury. Things had improved so much over the past week.

"You know," Paul mused, "I'm able to put a little weight on my right foot. I wonder if I could get back to playing basketball before the cast comes off."

"Balancing on one crutch while dribbling the ball with the other? In your dreams, mister."

She checked for traffic, then crossed Mountain Laurel Road. Paul swiveled in his seat when they passed the high-school parking lot, then looked back at Kate.

"You missed your turn."

She chuckled. "I was wondering when you'd catch on. I need to stop at the Mercantile first. The Faith Briar kids are running the concession stand at tonight's game, and I promised to donate some tortilla chips for nachos. I forgot to pick them up earlier. It won't take more than a couple of minutes."

She turned onto Main Street, pleased to find a parking spot in front of the Mercantile. "Go back to your daydreaming. I won't be long."

■ ■ ■ ■

It took only a few minutes to locate the tortilla chips in the snack aisle. Kate grabbed three of the large-sized bags and carried them toward the front of the store.

As she neared the register, she could hear the raspy voice of Arlene Jacobs, Sam Gorman's part-time cashier.

"You're thirty-five cents short. You have another quarter and a dime on you?"

Kate took her place in line and eyed one of the magazines on the nearby rack while the customer in front of her dug in the pockets of his brown bomber jacket.

Wait a minute. Kate blinked, then leaned to one side for a better look at his face. *Yes!* A tingle of electricity shot through her when she recognized the mystery boy who seemed to keep crossing her path.

He rummaged around in his pants pockets, then went back to searching in the jacket again. His slender face puckered, and he licked his lips. "I know I had more with me."

His face lit up. "Hey, I think there's a hole in my pocket."

Kate watched him ram his hands deeper into the jacket and saw his arm move across the back.

Arlene looked her way. "Sorry about the delay, Kate. Why don't I void this out and ring up your order while I'm waiting?"

The boy looked around and made eye contact. A dull red flush stained his cheeks. Kate smiled, telling herself not to be daunted by the flare of panic she could see in his eyes.

This made the fourth — or was it the fifth? — time she had come in contact with him in recent days. In her experience, there was no such thing as a coincidence.

No, God put this young man in her path for a reason. It was up to her to go along with the program, whatever that might be, and find out what she was supposed to do about it.

She looked down at the boy's purchases: a small package of string cheese, a Heath candy bar, and a pint of milk. Her heart went out to him. He needed to eat every bit of that, and a whole lot more. His brown leather jacket hung loose on his skinny frame.

Having watched Andrew and his friends while he was growing up, she knew all about teenage boys and their voracious appetites. But from the determination this one had not to miss out on buying this small assortment of groceries, she felt sure this food meant far more than just one more light snack to him.

She set the tortilla chips on the belt and shoved them toward the other items. "Just ring them up all together," she told Arlene.

She handed over the purchase price, then scooped up the milk, cheese, and the candy bar and held them out to the boy. "Here, this is on me."

He started to reach for the items, then pulled his hands back and shook his head. "I can't."

Kate didn't budge. "Come on. I've had the same thing happen to me before. I know how frustrating it is to think you have money and find out it's missing." He shook his head again.

"Do it for me," she added with a laugh. "It will let me feel like I've made up a little bit for practically running you down the other day."

The boy paused, then took the items with a casual air that belied his hungry look. "Thanks. I really appreciate it."

Kate watched the way he clung to the food and felt he was showing remarkable self-restraint in not tearing the wrapper off the cheese and shoving one of the sticks into his mouth right then.

"Thanks," he said again, smiling at her for the first time.

He had a nice smile, Kate thought. And a nice face, with those warm brown eyes and even, white teeth. It was the kind of face girls his age would swoon over.

Did girls still swoon? Probably not, Kate decided, but whatever the current day's reaction was called, she felt sure this boy would produce it.

Moreover, he had the kind of bearing — forthright but not overconfident — that would produce a feeling of trust in the girls' parents.

It was certainly working on her right then. Kate loved young people in general, but something about this one tugged at her heartstrings and made her want to do something to help him, even though she didn't know a thing about him or his needs.

Acting on impulse, Kate pulled a ten-dollar bill from her purse and held it out to him.

The boy jerked back as though she'd tried to hand him a West Texas rattler. As quickly as it had appeared, the smile dropped away.

"No." His tone told her he meant business. "I'm not looking for charity."

I was right. He is a nice boy. Kate folded the bill but kept it in her hand. "It isn't charity." She spoke in a brisk tone. "More like a business proposition."

He flickered a look at the exit. Kate touched his elbow and steered him outside before he could panic and take off again. "I'd like you to meet my husband. He's waiting right outside."

Without giving him time to respond, she led him out to her Honda.

Paul raised his eyebrows when she stepped into the street and circled around to the passenger side. Kate didn't offer any explanation, just motioned for him to roll down his window.

She beckoned for the boy to follow and gave Paul a look that meant, "Go along with me on this. I'll fill you in later."

"I think I've found an answer to your dilemma about the backyard."

Paul gave her a puzzled look, then his face cleared. "You mean those broken limbs?" At Kate's nod, he reached through the open window and extended his hand to Kate's confused companion.

"Paul Hanlon," he said. "I'm the pastor of Faith Briar Church."

To his credit, the young man responded without hesitation and grasped Paul's hand in a firm grip. "Nice to meet you, sir. My name's Cody."

Kate tucked that bit of information away in her memory. How nice to know his name at last!

Paul smiled. "You'll have to excuse me for not getting out to give you a proper greeting, but I have a bum leg at the moment."

He indicated the crutches angled across the back of the seat. "That's how you can help me out, if you're willing."

Cody squared his shoulders. "I'd be happy to help, if I can."

Paul's eyes crinkled at the corners. "Glad to hear it. An attitude like that will take you far. Here's the situation. That storm we had the other night knocked some limbs off one of our trees and broke more of them loose. They're just dangling from the trunk, and I don't want them to hurt anyone. With this leg the way it is, I'm not in any shape to cut them down and clear them away. Does that sound like something you'd be willing to tackle?"

Cody nodded eagerly. "Sure. No problem."

Kate held up her hand and fluttered her fingers so Paul could see the bill she held tucked in her palm.

Without missing a beat, he added, "We'll pay you for your time, of course."

The boy flushed. "That won't be necessary."

"Nonsense. A workman is worthy of his hire."

Kate seized the opportunity to press the ten-dollar bill into the boy's hand and closed his fingers around it. She smiled up at him. "See? I told you it wasn't charity."

Cody looked down at his hand, then shoved the cash into his front pocket as though he was afraid he might change his mind if he hesitated.

He looked back at Paul, and his brow furrowed. "I don't know where you live."

Paul motioned toward the backseat. "Hop in. We'll take you as far as the high school. It's only a little ways up the road from there. Oh, wait a minute. You're going to need a saw and a ladder."

He pulled out his key ring, separated one of the keys from the rest, and handed it to Cody. "This'll get you into the garage. There's a light switch by the back door. The tools are along the right-hand side. You'll find the pruning saw hanging on a rack on the wall. It's the one with the thin, curved blade."

Cody nodded. "I know what one looks like."

"Great. You'll need to cut off the limbs

that are hanging from the tree, and then saw all the downed branches into shorter lengths. When you're finished, I'd like you to carry them out of the yard and stack them all on the other side of the fence."

"I can do that, no problem." Cody turned the key over in his hands. "But are you sure you want to give me this? You don't even know me."

Paul gave him a wink. "My wife is a good judge of character. If she thinks you're the right one for the job, that's good enough for me."

After dropping Cody off at the high school, Kate eyed Paul skeptically. "I wanted to give him a chance to earn some money, but I didn't expect you to hand him your key right then and there."

"It's only the garage key. It won't let him into the house."

"But all your tools are in the garage. What if —"

Paul reached toward the steering wheel and covered her hand with his. "Sometimes you have to believe in people enough to let them believe in themselves. I have a feeling that if my actions show I trust this young man of yours, he'll rise to the occasion."

Kate pulled his hand to her lips long enough to press a kiss on his fingers. "That's one of the reasons I love you, Paul Hanlon."

CHAPTER NINETEEN

Kate cupped her chin in her hands and tried to tune out the sounds of pounding feet and a cheering crowd.

Did Avery have anything to do with the runaway Mustang? And did any kind of connection exist between him and Roland Myers? Those questions and more had plagued her ever since Skip's surprising statement three days earlier.

Now she had two leads to follow, if only she could find the time to pursue them!

A long stint in her studio the day before allowed her to make substantial progress on the fanlight. Perhaps she could spare an hour or two sometime in the next few days to —

"All *right!*" Paul clapped enthusiastically and pounded the front of the bleacher with his good foot.

Kate came back to the present with a jolt.

Paul beamed from ear to ear. "Wasn't that

a great play?"

Kate nodded and smiled, hoping she didn't appear as clueless as she felt. She slid closer to him on the bleacher and twined her arm through his.

Normally she preferred sitting about midway up in the stands so as to be able to see all the action. That evening they sat on the lowest bleacher so Paul wouldn't have to climb.

The view wasn't nearly as good without the advantage of height, but with Paul beside her, it didn't matter one bit. That Friday night she felt far more a part of things than at the last game she attended — and it was all due to having the security of his presence.

It did seem odd, though, to have Paul sitting next to her instead of being out on the court with the other Faith Briar players.

Looking at Paul, she suspected he felt the same way. He wore a broad smile and cheered for Faith Briar, adding his voice to the good-natured catcalls aimed at the players from St. Lucy's.

But years of marriage had taught her to read the subtle signs below the surface. Beneath his buoyant exterior, she could detect a slightly hollow note.

He had seemed happy enough when they

first arrived, smiling at all the people who came up to greet him and accepting claps on the back from teammates who said they knew a little thing like a broken ankle couldn't keep him away for long. But it wasn't the same as spending the evening out on the court as one of the players. Kate sensed the change in him the moment the opening buzzer sounded.

Sitting together as spectators wasn't anything new for them. They had joked about wearing the varnish thin on their accustomed spots in the bleachers during Andrew's high-school and college games. But this was different.

At Andrew's games, their role was that of proud parents supporting their son.

But on this particular night, it was Paul's team out there on the court, and Kate knew that made all the difference in the world. Paul's features were set in a wistful expression, like someone on the outside looking in.

Like Cody, she realized with a start.

She looked back at Paul, wondering if her imagination had been working overtime. No, she hadn't dreamed up the similarity. Paul wore a look of longing to be a part of things, to fit in — the same look she had seen more than once on Cody's face.

Kate's thoughts drifted to the boy who was clearing their yard of tree limbs at that moment. She had finally made a positive contact with him, but she still didn't know his story, his family, or anything about him.

When she came right down to it, she knew nothing at all except for being convinced that God had brought the teenager into her life for some purpose.

She closed her eyes, the better to tune out the game sounds around her. *Father, help me to know what that purpose is. I haven't done so well with him up to now, knocking him into walls and scaring him away.*

"Way to go, Justin!" Paul shouted. He pounded on the seat with his left hand and squeezed Kate's arm with his right. "That's the way to block a shot!"

Kate returned the squeeze, feeling a surge of appreciation for her husband.

How grateful she felt for Paul's unquestioning support and quick understanding of her plan to win Cody's confidence. Mere seconds after meeting Paul, the boy seemed at ease for the first time since she'd bumped into him.

She wouldn't press too hard, she told herself, falling back into her reverie. She didn't want to frighten him off just when she was starting to make progress.

At least she seemed to have made some inroads. Kate snuggled closer to Paul while she enumerated them. For one thing, she knew Cody's name at last.

But not his last name, she realized with a pang of disappointment. Still, it was something to go on. She didn't have to keep referring to him in her thoughts as "that boy" anymore.

For another, she sensed an immediate connection between him and Paul. She felt so grateful the two of them had finally met. Kate smiled and sent up another quick prayer. *Forgetting those tortilla chips was no accident after all, was it, Lord?*

Third, there was Cody's willingness to pitch in and help a couple of total strangers. Another indication of his good character.

So she did know a little about him after all. But what was the next step?

Kate pondered the question. Now that Cody had lost his nervousness around her, she would try to engage him in a conversation the next time she saw him.

And there would be a next time. After all the times their paths had crossed already, she had no doubt it would happen again. And she intended to be ready when it did.

Her mind raced ahead, making plans.

Since Cody now knew where they lived, maybe he would feel comfortable coming over to visit if she invited him to join her and Paul for some cookies.

Thinking of Andrew and his friends, she felt sure the ploy would work. Remembering their hollow legs, maybe she ought to make a double batch. No, make that an assortment of several varieties.

Kate lost herself in sorting through her favorite recipes. She would make chocolate chip and oatmeal raisin for sure. And maybe some peanut-butter cookies. Andrew's friends had always clamored for those.

Blaaatttt! Kate jumped at the sound of the buzzer. A quick look at the clock told her the game was over.

Already? She shot a guilty look in Paul's direction and saw him clapping wildly. At least she could tell from his reaction that the Faith Briar team had won.

Paul gathered up his crutches and made his way across the court to congratulate his teammates and trade friendly gibes with the opposing coach.

"Great game!" Kate could hear his booming voice above the rest of the noise.

They stayed until Paul had congratulated every one of his team members. Kate followed his lead as he waved good-bye and made his way out to the parking lot, thinking how odd it felt not to stay around until he and his teammates emerged from the locker room.

"Quite a game, wasn't it?"

"It was, indeed." Kate hoped he wouldn't expect her to remember any details. She didn't want to admit she'd been so wrapped up in her own thoughts that she couldn't even tell him the final score.

"A good game," Paul repeated when he had settled into the passenger seat of the Honda. "They all did a fine job."

Kate knew his pleasure was genuine but sensed he felt slightly wounded that the team had been able to win without his help.

She started the engine, suddenly anxious to get home so she could sort through the thoughts that had occurred to her during the game. More than ever, she felt compelled to discover who took that Mustang, especially since Sheriff Roberts seemed inclined to write it off as a lost cause.

Not only that, she needed time to mull over the possibility of Avery's involvement and decide what to do about it.

Before she could put the Honda in gear, Paul's team started filtering out of the gym. "Looks like they're heading over to the Smokeshack," he said.

Kate heard the tinge of sadness in his voice. The man needed cheering up, even if it meant delaying her own plans.

"How about joining them?" She guided the Honda across the parking lot. "I know they'd be thrilled if you could come."

Paul waited a beat before answering. "I think I'd rather get home and see how that young man got along."

Kate didn't argue, though she suspected his real reason had more to do with not wanting to feel like the odd man out than any concern about the quality of Cody's work.

Her heart went out to him; she looked forward to the day when he would be feeling like himself again. She put on her left blinker and slowed to turn onto Smoky Mountain Road.

"Wait a minute." Paul sat up straighter, an excited look on his face. "I've just had an idea. Turn around and head back into town, will you? I didn't see Eli at the game tonight, and I need to talk to him."

Chapter Twenty

Kate swung the steering wheel back to the right and turned onto Smoky Mountain Road, crossing Mountain Laurel and heading toward Hamilton. The car shifted through its gears smoothly.

She only wished her thought processes could change speeds with such ease.

But she would manage. A smile curved her lips. Being a pastor's wife all these years had taught her to expect the unexpected.

She made a right turn on Hamilton, then a left on Smith Street, and pulled up to the curb in front of Weston's Antiques. Lights shone in Eli's living quarters upstairs.

"It looks like he's home. Do you want me to make sure before you climb out of the car?"

"No, let's go together. I need all the exercise I can get."

Kate went ahead of him, past the white picket fence and up the brick walkway to the front porch, thankful for the scrolled gas street lamps flanking the front steps that lit her way.

She pressed the doorbell, her thoughts already moving ahead. As soon as she had Paul situated inside, she could go back to her car and sort through her thoughts about Avery and the diner mystery.

From inside the building, she could hear the sound of footsteps descending the stairs. One edge of the lace curtains at the front window drew back, and Eli's face peered around it.

"It's Paul and Kate," she called, uncertain of how well Eli could see through his tortoise-shell glasses in the dark.

The curtain dropped back into place before she finished speaking. She waved for Paul to join her. A moment later, Eli stood in the doorway, a smile of welcome on his lips.

"What a pleasant surprise! Come on inside."

Paul leaned on his crutches. "We don't mean to intrude on your evening, but I wonder if you might have a few minutes to talk."

"Of course." Eli ushered them inside and closed the door.

Paul shrugged out of his coat and hung it

on a hall tree near the entrance. "I just wanted to run an idea past you and see if you think it would be worthwhile."

"Sure." Eli's shy smile lit his whole face. "I'm always glad to help."

Kate edged toward the door. "Why don't I wait in the car and give you some privacy?"

"Not on a cold night like this," Eli protested. "Paul and I can go in my office. Why don't you browse around the store while we talk? I have some new items you might be interested in looking at."

Kate hesitated. "Is this going to take quite a while?"

"Probably not," Paul said. "But Eli's right. It's cold out there. I'd feel better if you stayed inside where you'll be warm."

The two men disappeared around a corner, and Kate heard the click of the door to Eli's office. She sighed, hoping whatever Paul planned to discuss wouldn't take too long.

Right now all she really wanted to do was to get home, curl up with a mug of coffee, and see if she could put together the pieces of this puzzle and come up with some answers.

She wandered through the rows of collectibles that made up the display area of Weston's Antiques. It looked as if Eli had added a couple of rolltop desks to his inventory since she had been in there last.

Kate threaded between a familiar serpentine-back sofa and a rosewood wardrobe and angled toward a walnut drop-front secretary. She didn't see anything different in this part of the store.

Over in the corner, a stately grandfather clock ticked away, reminding her of the passing minutes. Much as she usually enjoyed looking at antiques, that night she longed for nothing more than to be alone with her thoughts.

Kate tapped her fingers against the carving on the back of a rocking chair that had belonged to some child from the Victorian era. She knew Paul wouldn't have come to see Eli without a good reason. And experience had taught her there were no set hours for a pastor's work.

Still, it would be nice to be able to look forward to an evening at home without any distractions.

On the other hand, she would never want to trade places with anyone. The joys of being a minister's wife far outweighed any of the apparent inconveniences.

Look at the ways God had used them already in Copper Mill. The move had been a good one for Paul . . . even if he was on crutches at the moment.

Kate looked toward the back of the store, longing to hear the office door open.

Nothing yet.

She sighed again and headed for the area where Eli displayed some of the more fragile items. Maybe she could find a new teapot for her collection.

That foray ended in disappointment. Nothing new had been added to his assortment of teapots since her last shopping tour.

Kate fidgeted, wondering how much longer their discussion would take. *And men say women talk a lot!*

Over in a corner, she spied an old friend, a Tiffany lamp Eli purchased at an estate sale. No matter how often she saw the elegant creation, Kate felt drawn toward it.

It wouldn't hurt to go look at it one more time. She never tired of studying the craftsman's technique, looking for ways to improve her own stained-glass skills.

Just past a mahogany game table, a marble-topped dresser blocked her way. Kate didn't remember seeing it before. It must have been one of the new pieces Eli mentioned.

She started to circle around it, noting the various items laying on its shiny surface as she passed: a tortoise-shell comb and brush set, several pieces of Victorian hairwork jewelry, and a ceramic hair receiver.

Kate smiled at the picture forming in her mind of the woman whose nightly ritual involved collecting the loose hair the brush had removed and stuffing it through the hole in the top of the hair receiver, storing it there until she had enough to braid it into a decorative brooch.

At the other end of the dresser lay . . . Kate caught her breath when she recognized an old stereoscope. She squeezed past a walnut chest of drawers to reach it.

Picking up the fragile piece with tender care, she turned it over in her hands, delighted to see that all its parts were in place. She held it up to the light and examined the design pressed into the tin hood.

"Just like Gran's." She let out a happy sigh.

At the edge of the dresser, she spied a stack of stereographs. Feeling like a little girl searching through her grandma's treasures, Kate sorted through them.

She found one set of pictures of a lion tamer at a Ringling Brothers Circus performance, another of immigrants arriving at Ellis Island.

Setting those aside, she picked up a card

showing the Ferris wheel at the 1893 World's Columbian Exposition in Chicago and slipped it into the wire slots in the holder.

Gripping the handle underneath, she held the device so the light fell squarely on the photos, then looked through the lenses and moved the holder back and forth. A tremble of excitement shivered through her when the pictures popped into focus and merged into a three-dimensional scene.

And this is what they used for entertainment back then. Kate shook her head. What would the people of that day have thought about television, movies, and the Internet?

"Find something you can't live without?"

Kate jumped when Paul's voice boomed in her ear. She turned and held up the stereoscope for him to see.

"You'd better be glad I had a good grip on this, or you'd be paying Eli for it right now."

Eli chuckled. "If you're planning on buying that, Paul, I'd rather it was in one piece. It's a much better buy if you're able to get some enjoyment out of it."

He turned to Kate. "You looked like you were enjoying yourself."

"More than you know." Kate returned the stereoscope to its spot on the dresser. "It was like a little walk down memory lane. My grandmother owned one like this, and I've always been fascinated by the way the two pictures come together to form one with so much depth."

"I had a toy that worked along the same lines when I was a kid." Eli stroked the stereoscope with his fingertips, looking for all the world like a proud father gazing down at a favorite offspring. "But nothing beats the original, in my opinion. Are you interested in buying it?"

Kate looked at the product of nineteenth-century technology, seized by a sudden longing to return to a time when life didn't seem so complex. But had there ever been such a time? Every generation had its own difficulties to cope with.

She traced the pressed design, marveling at how well it had stood up over the passage of time. "I'll have to think about it."

Eli nodded affably. "Just let me know. I'm always happy when a buyer knows how to appreciate a purchase."

Kate smiled up at the men. "Have you finished talking?"

"We have indeed." Paul turned to Eli and shook the younger man's hand. "Thanks for your input. We'll discuss it more next week."

He and Kate retraced their steps to the

front door and said their good-byes.

In the car, Paul filled her in on the details of their impromptu visit.

"An idea popped into my head while you went inside the Mercantile for tortilla chips. I wanted to run it past Eli while it was still fresh in my mind."

He shifted in his seat so he could face her more directly. "There are still a number of people who aren't happy with me for giving Avery the job at the church."

Kate gripped the steering wheel tighter. As if Paul needed to deal with something like this, on top of his injury!

Paul held up one hand. "Don't get upset. They have a right to their opinions. I'm their shepherd, not their dictator."

Kate took a calming breath and counted to ten. "Okay, so what was your idea?"

"I haven't given up on Avery. I'm still determined to help him, but I don't want this whole situation to blow up out of proportion and turn into something hurtful. So here's what came to mind: I want to keep Avery on at the church, but I'd like to have someone else supervise his work, a neutral third party who doesn't have any preconceived notions to color his judgment."

Kate considered the plan, nodding as the idea took hold. "That's brilliant. That way nobody can say you're covering up or trying to make things easy for him."

"That's exactly the way I look at it. And I thought Eli would be the ideal person to take that on. He's had his own problems, goodness knows. After starting the fire that burned Faith Briar to the ground the day we arrived in Copper Mill, he knows what it's like to have a black mark on his record."

"And to be forgiven and accepted in spite of past failures," Kate added. "It sounds like a perfect solution. What did he say?"

She could see Paul's smile in the glow of the dashboard. "He told me exactly what I wanted to hear. He's interested, but he wants to pray about it first. He'll let me know next Sunday."

Kate's eyes misted, and she blinked to clear her vision. "It's a real joy to watch him mature spiritually. You've really had an impact on him, Paul."

"Don't sell your own influence short. You've had a part in it too." He squeezed her arm gently. "We make a good team."

Kate threw him a smile as she turned into their driveway and pushed the button on the remote to open the garage door. "I couldn't agree more."

She pulled into the garage and turned off the ignition. Paul stepped out of the Honda with more dexterity than he had shown in days. The sight warmed Kate. He really was on the mend.

As if to prove her point, he rounded the front of the car and moved ahead of her to open the door to the house.

"Let's see what the backyard looks like. I keep thinking how nice it's going to be to look out the window and not see those limbs lying every which way."

They walked straight through the foyer to the living room, turned on the outside porch light, and stepped through the sliding-glass doors. A relieved sigh escaped Kate's lips at the sight of the backyard looking neat and trim once more.

The limbs had been removed from the trees with a fair amount of skill, and the pile that formerly littered the yard had been carted off, presumably to the spot behind the fence.

Paul gave an approving nod. "He did a good job."

"Didn't he? It looks like he even raked up the loose twigs."

"You were right, Katie. He seems like a fine young man, although you can tell he has something pretty heavy weighing on his mind."

"I've felt that from the very beginning." Kate looked up and grinned. "You aren't the only one who came up with a plan tonight."

She filled him in on her intention to invite Cody over to their house for cookies.

"I thought it might be a way to make him feel safer around us and give the two of you a chance to get better acquainted." She nudged Paul with her elbow. "And you know what they say about the way to a man's heart."

"It's always worked for me." He pulled Kate close and rubbed his cheek against her hair. "That's a great idea, hon. I hope we'll be able to find a way to help him. And you know I'm always open to an excuse to indulge in your cookies."

His voice took on a hopeful note. "I don't suppose your plan includes a batch of lemon squares?"

Kate laughed and tousled his hair with her fingers. "I might be persuaded to add them to the list."

"That's my girl." He reached to open the slider again, then snapped his fingers. "I meant to check and see if he left the key on the workbench."

Kate moved past him. "I'll go look."

She returned to the living room a few moments later. "Paul, you'll never guess . . ."

"Don't tell me. He didn't leave the key where I told him to."

"Oh, he left it all right. Your saw and ladder are back in place too, but he left something besides the key. Look what I found with it on the workbench." She held out her hand to show him a folded ten-dollar bill.

Paul reached out and took it from her. He unfolded the crisp paper and smoothed out the creases. "Do you think he just forgot it?"

Kate shook her head. "It wasn't just tossed down by accident. The key was set right on top of it. Why didn't he take it? He was adamant about not taking charity, but this was honest payment for honest work. He obviously needed the money, so why would he leave it behind?"

"Maybe he felt your buying the snack for him was payment enough. Evidently, someone has instilled a sense of integrity in that boy."

"I can't get past the feeling that he needs our help in some way." Kate raised her hands, then dropped them to her sides. "But how are we supposed to help if we can't get close enough to him to find out what's wrong?"

Paul pulled the curtains closed across the slider. "We'll have to approach this like so many other things in life: one step at a time."

"You're right, I know. I just have this feeling that something needs to be done now." Kate let her breath out in a long sigh. "I'd better fix us something to eat. What sounds good to you?"

Paul glanced at his watch. "It's nearly ten o'clock, way too late for you to be fixing a full meal. I'm not very hungry anyway. I think I'll just grab a sandwich and read in bed for a while. Is that okay with you?"

Kate gave him a quick hug and chuckled. "As long as you don't get crumbs on the sheets. If you don't mind, I think I'll eat out here. I'd like to sit up for a while."

She fixed sandwiches and cocoa for both of them, then carried Paul's plate and mug to the bedroom. Kate settled down at the kitchen table with her light meal, free at last to focus her attention on the Mustang mystery.

Where to start? Kate smiled. At the beginning, just as Livvy said. She would approach this the same way she would assemble a jigsaw puzzle: group the similar pieces, then fit them together one by one until a picture emerged.

She retrieved the list of points she'd made after the accident along with her sketch of the crime scene and stared at them as if they held the answers. She had most of the pieces she needed, she felt sure of that. All she had to do at this point was to see which pieces fit together and keep moving them around until they formed a picture that made sense.

But after only a few sips of cocoa, she found herself propping her chin up on one hand, trying to stay awake, while thoughts of the Mustang, her wallet, Roland Myers, Avery, Cody, and the ten-dollar bill whirled through her mind.

Her head drooped lower, and her eyelids grew heavy.

Kate startled awake and blinked, trying to remember where she was. She rubbed her eyes and shook her head. It was no use trying to force logical thought from a sleep-fogged brain. With a sigh of resignation, she gathered up her dishes and set them in the sink.

She would go back to work on the puzzle the following morning when her mind was fresh.

Chapter Twenty-One

The bell jingled merrily over the door of Smith Street Gifts. Steve Smith looked up and waved from the back of the store.

"Hey, Kate! How's that fanlight coming?"

"I'm making good progress." *Finally,* she added to herself. Each passing day found Paul able to get around better on his own, leaving her with more time to devote to working in her studio.

She set a cardboard tube down on the counter next to the register and pulled the cap off one end. "I thought you might like to see this."

Steve joined her, watching as she slipped a roll of paper from the tube and spread it out across the glass-topped display case. He whistled as he examined the color sketch from several angles.

"This is the design you've come up with for the fanlight?"

Kate nodded, encouraged by the appreciative light in his eyes.

"It's nice. Really impressive." He looked down at the sketch again, then back up at Kate. "When do you think it'll be ready?"

"Why don't you give me another week or so, just to be on the safe side? I shouldn't have any problem delivering it to you by then."

"That'll be great. I expect Mr. Michaels to be coming through town around that time. I'll call and let him know he can pick it up then. He's going to be one happy customer."

Steve leaned back and braced his elbows against the counter. "How's Paul doing?"

"He's coming along well. His ankle seems to be healing nicely." Kate rolled up the sketch and replaced it in the cardboard tube. "Since he broke his right ankle, I'm still doing all the driving. But he's walking without using his crutches now, and it looks like he's well on his way to recovery. The doctor says he'll be good as new in a few weeks, *if* he behaves himself," she added with a chuckle.

"Getting a little impatient, is he?" Laugh lines crinkled at the corners of Steve's eyes. "I guess you just can't keep a good man down."

The bell jangled again, and Emma Blount,

the owner of Emma's Ice Cream, burst through the door.

"Has anyone seen Jennifer McCarthy? I didn't get any answer when I called the *Chronicle* office."

Steve glanced at Kate, who shook her head.

"Sorry," he said. "What's up?"

Emma pressed her hand against her chest and gasped for breath. "She needs to bring her camera and get herself down the street right quick so she can get some good photos before it's all over."

Steve's forehead crinkled. "Before what's all over? What's gotten into you, Emma?"

"The protest!" She waved her arms wildly. "We're having one of those demonstrations like you see on TV, right here in Copper Mill!"

She rushed back outside before Steve or Kate could pose another question.

The door hissed shut. Before it closed completely, the sound of a boisterous crowd of people filtered inside the shop.

Kate stared at Steve. "A demonstration? What on earth is she talking about?"

Steve shook his head emphatically. "Something's wrong. That just can't be right. Things like that don't happen in Copper Mill." He strode toward the door, with Kate at his heels.

The volume of the voices increased the moment he opened the door. Kate slipped past him and peered down the street in the direction Emma had headed. The sight that met her eyes reminded her of a scene from the sixties.

A throng of people spilled off the sidewalk onto Smith Street up near the corner of Hamilton Road. A number of them carried homemade picket signs. Kate could hear them chanting as they walked in a slow circle in front of the Country Diner.

Kate took a second look. What appeared to be a sizable crowd at first probably didn't add up to more than twenty or twenty-five people. A minuscule gathering by big-city standards, but enough to look like a threatening mob in this small-town setting.

Protesters in Copper Mill? What on earth? Kate tried to pick out what the marchers were saying but couldn't catch more than a few stray syllables.

Overwhelmed by curiosity, she joined the others who flocked toward the scene. Eli's truck pulled up just ahead of her and stopped long enough to let Paul step out of the passenger side.

With a surge of relief, Kate rushed over to him. "What's going on?"

Paul's mouth set in a firm line. "That's a good question. Loretta called me and said a whole mob was marching on the diner. I couldn't reach you on your cell phone, so I called Eli and asked him to bring me down here to find out what was happening. He's gone to park around back and make sure everything in his store is secure."

He rubbed his hand across the top of his head. "I thought she was overreacting, but this . . ." He gestured toward the marchers and shook his head.

"Come on." Kate tugged at his arm. "Let's go find out what's happening."

Paul pulled her back. "There's no telling what we'd be getting into. I think you'd better stay here until we know what this is all about."

"And miss all the excitement? I don't think so." She raised her chin. "We're a team, remember?"

Paul looked at her for a long moment, then nodded. Together, they approached the diner. They paused at the edge of the crowd, and Kate nudged him, grinning. "I don't think we're looking at an unruly mob here. Do you see those signs?"

Paul stopped short as they stared at the unlikely scene playing out in front of them.

It looked like the protesters had bought

out every sheet of fluorescent poster board the SuperMart in Pine Ridge had in stock. Heavy block letters printed with black felt markers proclaimed the protesters' sentiments:

Bring Back Our Sweet-Potato Fries!

We Love You, Loretta!

Don't Sell Out!!!

Grits, yes! Quiche, *non!*

"Oh my!" Kate pressed her hand against her lips, not certain whether she should laugh or cry.

Paul moved ahead with as much grace as a man wearing a moon boot could muster. Kate recovered her composure enough to follow.

He stopped directly in front of the diner and raised his hands. "Hey, folks, does anybody want to tell me what's going on here? You've got Loretta scared to death."

Bit by bit, the rumble of the crowd faded to silence.

Kate heard a rustling sound behind him, and Loretta's head poked out between the heavy tarps that draped the front of the building.

"I'm not scared, I'm mad! What's wrong with you people? Don't you gotta have a permit if you're gonna block traffic like that?"

As soon as the words left her mouth, she disappeared, and the tarps swished back into place. From behind the protective covering, Kate heard the distinct click of a lock.

Paul watched the tarps as if expecting her to return at any moment, then he turned back to the crowd.

"Okay, you've gotten Loretta's attention. Why don't you all head home now?"

Lester Philpott lowered his sign demanding the return of the sweet-potato fries. "We don't mean any harm, Pastor. It's all in good fun. We just want Loretta to know how much we love the diner."

"Right," called Willy Bergen, owner of Willy's Bait and Tackle. "But we'd like some answers, just the same. She's got the whole building closed up tight so we can't tell what's going on inside. But there's a work crew going in and out every day. We want to know what's going on."

"That's right." Kate recognized the grits fancier as Ronda, one of the young stylists at Betty's. "Someone told me she's just fixin' the place up so she can sell it and move to one of those fancy retirement resorts in Florida."

A chorus of "Nooooo!" rose from the crowd, followed by cries of, "Don't do it, Loretta! You can't leave us. We need you here!"

As if obeying an unseen signal, the group started marching again, chanting in unison. This time Kate was close enough to hear every word: "Hey, hey, ho, ho. We won't let our diner go!"

Paul shook his head and spoke quietly so only Kate could hear. "I should have realized Loretta wasn't really in a panic when she called me instead of the sheriff. Still, I think this has gone on long enough."

"Listen up!" Paul raised his voice to be heard over the clamor and affected a stern demeanor, though Kate could tell he was trying hard not to laugh. "What do you think this is going to accomplish? You've taken out an ad in the *Chronicle.* You've rung Loretta's phone off the hook and worn a path to her front door. And now you're demonstrating?"

He gestured at the brilliant rainbow of protest signs. "You've made your point. If you really want to keep the diner open, Loretta needs to be free to make that decision because it's what *she* wants to do, not because she's being coerced into doing it."

With sheepish expressions, most of the crowd lowered their signs and started to move away.

One disgruntled demonstrator flung back a parting shot: "You're a fine one to talk. We wouldn't be in this mess if it hadn't been for your wife driving that car through the front of the diner."

In all the years of their marriage, Kate could remember only a few times when she had seen Paul reduced to a state of speechlessness. This was one of them.

He stared after the departing group, gaping like one of the trout he and Sam Gorman liked to reel in from Copper Mill Creek.

When the last protester had gone, he turned around and stared at Kate. "Did I hear what I think I just heard?"

Kate walked over to him and slid her arm around his waist. It was one thing for Bernie the mechanic and his pals to think she had something to do with destroying the diner. It was a whole different matter to hear it spoken out loud in a public place.

"I'm afraid so." She leaned her head against his shoulder. "And all because my wallet turned up someplace it wasn't supposed to be."

She heard a soft click, followed by a rustle.

"Are they gone?"

Paul stepped over to the narrowed opening where Loretta's lined face peered out from between the tarps. "All gone. You can calm down now."

He reached out and started to push the tarp aside, but Loretta swatted at his hand. "Nope. Nobody's seeing the inside of this place until I've done what I'm going to do. Not even you."

Paul shoved his fingers through his hair. "You know, you'd save yourself and everybody else a lot of trouble if you'd just tell them what you're doing."

"It's my decision, isn't it?" Loretta jutted out her chin.

"Of course, but —"

"Then that's the way it's going to be. I have my reasons, and I'm not talkin'."

Before Paul could say another word, Loretta did her disappearing act again, followed by the swish of the tarp and a decisive *click* that told them the conversation was over.

Kate stared at Paul, who stared at the blank expanse of black plastic.

Finally he turned and gave her a look that reminded her of the time Andrew got a concussion playing high-school football.

"Where did you park your car?" he asked. "I think it's time to go home."

"It's just down the street. Stay right here. I'll pick you up in a jiffy." Kate hurried down Smith Street to retrieve her Honda, the keys jingling in her hand.

As humorous as the "demonstration" had turned out to be, one thing was clear: she had dithered long enough. Now it was time to take action. Her resolve grew firmer with every step she took.

It was bad enough to be the target of the local rumor mill. But now the wagging tongues had drawn Paul in as well.

She reached the Honda, flung open the door, and climbed behind the wheel. She started the engine, a single thought burning in her mind.

Too many questions were floating around Copper Mill. It was time to find some answers.

Chapter Twenty-Two

Several fruitless days later, Kate felt like she'd been beating her head against a wall. Figuratively, of course. But at the moment, doing it literally didn't sound like such a bad idea.

She piloted the Honda along Mountain Laurel Road on the way back toward town with one hand, holding the other up to shield her eyes from the slanting rays of the late-afternoon sun.

As long as the sheriff remained convinced the theft of the Mustang was the work of a transient who had long since left the area, she couldn't expect much activity from that quarter.

Remembering comments she overheard the night of the crash about a bunch of joyriding kids being responsible, Kate had talked to the teens in the Faith Briar youth group to see if they had heard anything along that line.

None of them knew anything — at least none who would admit it to the minister's wife if they did.

In an effort to do something — *anything* — to bring the case to a close, Kate had just made another trip out to Roland Myers' place. Unfortunately, that foray met the same fruitless end as her other efforts of late.

Her repeated knocks on his ramshackle front door brought no response, and Kate couldn't be sure whether that meant the Mustang's owner was away from home or avoiding her.

Kate cruised along the stretch of road where Mountain Laurel ran parallel to Copper Mill Creek. She glanced down at the speedometer and immediately eased her foot off the accelerator.

It wouldn't do to get a speeding ticket and allow her mounting frustration to cause more problems than she already had.

She leaned back against the seat and squinted against the sun. Something would break soon. It just had to. She shot a prayer heavenward. *Father, you already know what's happened here. Help me see what I'm missing.*

Based on the success of her previous sleuthing, she thought she'd have the puzzle all figured out by now. She'd done remarkably well at solving problems for others. What made this case so different?

It shouldn't be this hard.

She had already taken more time than she should from her work on the fanlight, meaning she would have to work extra hard that week to have it finished by the date promised.

Kate guided her car around a bend in the road, grateful for the brief respite from the glaring sun. The mystery had so preoccupied her mind, she hadn't even had a chance to track Cody down and invite him over for cookies.

She would have to rectify that as soon as she had a moment to spare. That might be a while, though. Lately it felt like she had pressure bearing down on her from a dozen different directions at once.

And Paul, the poor man, had been so patient. It couldn't have been easy for him, trying to deal with not being able to do everything for himself while she was out running errands hither and yon.

What a guy! She would have to do something special soon to show him how much she appreciated him.

And she knew just what that would be.

Kate slowed to make the right turn onto

Smoky Mountain Road, then changed course and continued down Mountain Laurel to Sweetwater Street instead. She would pick up a take-out meal from JD's Smokeshack. If she knew Paul, the taste of barbecue would be enough to make up for any amount of neglect.

And if she didn't have to cook, she ought to be able to squeeze in another hour in the studio that night. She pulled into the Smokeshack's parking lot, feeling virtuous at the idea of killing two birds with one stone.

Ten minutes later, she returned to her car, bearing an armload of bags containing barbecue sandwiches, curly fries, and cole-slaw. Humming a favorite old hymn, she headed back toward their house.

Halfway there, she remembered she had promised to pick up a commentary Paul needed from his church office. She smacked her hand against the steering wheel. If she took time to stop now, the food would get cold.

No, it wouldn't take all that long if she just ran inside the church, got the book, and came straight back out again. Millie didn't work there in the afternoons, so she wouldn't get caught talking.

She passed the corner of Smoky Mountain

Road for the second time and pulled up in front of the church building.

Avery's rattletrap pickup sat back near the storage shed. Kate's brows knit together. This wasn't his regular cleaning day. What could he be doing at the church?

Her hand hovered over the ignition, wondering if she ought to go home and bring Paul back with her. Her fingers closed around the key when she heard someone call out a greeting. Looking around for the source, she finally spotted Avery kneeling on the roof.

He pushed himself upright and walked over to the edge. "Afternoon, Miz Hanlon."

She got out and walked toward him, shielding her eyes with her hand. "Hello there. I just stopped by to get something Paul needed. Is there a problem with the roof?"

Avery grinned and held up a claw hammer. "There won't be for long. That storm blew some shingles off. I wanted to put some new ones on before we get any more weather."

Relief at knowing he had a legitimate reason for being there made Kate feel lightheaded. She smiled up at him.

"Do you have everything you need?"

"I'm in fine shape, thanks. There were

some extra shingles in the storage shed where we keep the lawn mower, and I brought some roofing nails from home."

"The lawn mower?" Remembering what Millie had told Eli about the mower's disappearance, Kate tried to adopt a casual tone. "Someone said they looked for it the other day, but it wasn't in its usual place. Do you have any idea where it is?"

Avery's eyes crinkled when he smiled. "It's right back where it belongs. I put it there myself this morning."

He chuckled at Kate's puzzled look.

"I spotted a dove's nest with two eggs in it a couple of weeks ago. They don't usually build their nests until sometime in March, so it looks like we're due for an early spring. I took a look at the mower to make sure it'd be ready when we need it. The engine sounded okay, but the blades needed sharpening, so I took it home to go over it and give it a good tune-up while I was at it. It's all ready to go as soon as we need it."

Kate couldn't hold back a smile. Wouldn't Paul be relieved to learn why Avery had driven off with the lawn mower! "It sounds like you're on top of things, so I'll leave you to your work. Replacing those shingles sounds like quite a job."

"It won't take all that long. I've done it

often enough out at my place, and today I've even got me a helper."

Kate's gaze swept the otherwise empty parking lot. She turned a quizzical look on Avery.

He laughed and called out in the direction of the bell tower. "Come on out here before the preacher's wife thinks I'm seein' things."

Kate heard a shuffling sound, then saw Cody emerge from behind the steeple. He waved and gave her a shy grin.

Kate's spirits lifted even more. "Cody! How nice to see you."

"That's what I said." Avery's grin grew wider. "I was up here poundin' away, and who should come along and offer to help? It makes a big difference having him here. I'm gonna finish up a lot faster with him runnin' up and down the ladder whenever I need something."

He beamed at the boy like a proud parent. "He's a right good hand with a hammer too."

Kate noted the way Cody's cheeks flushed at the stream of compliments Avery poured out. She wondered how often the boy received such lavish praise.

"Well, we'd better get back to work." Avery fished in his pocket and tossed his key ring to Cody. "We're gonna need some more shingles pretty soon. How about loading them in the back of my truck and bringing it over by the ladder?"

Cody snagged the keys in midair, and his face turned pale. "No. I mean, I'd rather not."

Avery took the refusal in stride and retrieved the keys from the boy. "No problem. I'll just get them myself."

Cody pulled a hammer from the waistband of his jeans, looking relieved. "I'll finish up with the ones I was working on."

Kate carried the image of the boy bent diligently over his work as she went up the church steps and unlocked the front door. What was it about him that tugged at her heart so?

He was helpful, honest, and hardworking. Most kids his age would be sitting at home in front of a video game, not volunteering to do manual labor.

She searched the bookshelf and desk in Paul's office before she located the commentary in the bottom desk drawer. Pulling the bulky volume into her arms, she locked the office door behind her.

Her thoughts turned back to the teen on the roof.

Where did he get the energy to work as

hard as he did? He looked like he hadn't eaten a decent meal in days. Here was her chance to invite him over for cookies.

No, he needed something more substantial than cookies.

Wait a minute . . . She hurried back to deposit the commentary in her car.

Returning with an armload of barbecue, she saw Avery just getting out of his truck in the front parking lot. Kate walked over to the pickup and held out the bags, careful not to look in Cody's direction.

Avery reached out for one of the bags and took an appreciative whiff. "What's this?"

"I know what hard work does for a man's appetite. I wouldn't want you to be reduced to doing any more foraging in the refrigerator."

Avery burst out laughing. "I can tell you right now, I won't be tempted to do that again for a long, long time. Thanks a lot, Miz Hanlon. I really appreciate it."

Kate started back to her car. When she got halfway there, she called in a casual but clearly audible voice, "There should be plenty for both of you, if Cody's interested in eating too."

The last thing she saw as she drove away was the sight of Cody climbing down the ladder and making a beeline for Avery.

■ ■ ■ ■

"I wish you could have seen how excited he looked at the thought of getting a hot meal."

Kate removed the wrappers from the sandwiches she picked up on her return visit to the Smokeshack and set them out on the plates she'd laid on the table.

Paul spooned a hearty helping of coleslaw beside his sandwich and reached for the curly fries. After a brief blessing, he looked over at her. "You don't have any idea where he lives or who he belongs to?"

Kate shook her head and fortified herself with a long sip of coffee. "He just seems to appear out of nowhere. No one I've talked to knows anything about him. Not even Lu-Anne. I asked Livvy to try to find out more the next time he shows up at the library, but she says he hasn't stopped by in days."

She drew in a deep breath and blew it out in a long sigh.

Paul set the sandwich down and clasped her fingers in his. "This is really bothering you, isn't it?"

An embarrassed laugh escaped Kate's lips. "I feel like I'm losing my touch. For the life of me, I can't figure out who this boy is, and after all this time, I still don't have the slightest idea who took Roland Myers' Mustang."

She picked at the coleslaw on her plate. "Ever since we moved to Copper Mill, I felt like God had opened up a whole new chapter in my life and given me a special talent for solving little mysteries. But maybe I was wrong."

Paul looked at her seriously. "You can hardly say you've lost your touch, Katie. You've just had your mind focused on too many things at once. Not to mention having to play nursemaid to an old cripple," he added with a grin.

"You haven't had the time to do more than give superficial attention to Cody with everything else that's been going on. When things let up enough so you can truly concentrate, I'm sure you'll find out everything you need to know."

Kate swallowed a bite of her barbecue sandwich, then blotted her lips on her napkin and leaned toward Paul.

"You know how sometimes you feel like God is putting you right in the middle of a situation, and it's critical that you do the right thing? That your actions have the potential to make a huge difference? Well, that's how I feel about this. But I don't know what the right thing is! That's what makes it so frustrating."

She cradled her coffee mug in her hands, struck by a sudden thought. "Do you think he comes from an abusive situation of some kind?"

Paul's face took on the pensive look he got when he was turning an idea over in his mind. "That would explain a lot — the way he keeps to himself, his hesitancy about giving out his name or any information about himself or his family."

"And why he looked so startled and scared when I first ran into him." Tears welled up in Kate's eyes. "I'll bet that's it, Paul! He needs help; I know it. What can we do?"

Paul rested his forearms on the table and tented his fingers. "Let's not jump to conclusions. On the other hand, look at the way he pitched in to help Avery without being asked. That isn't the norm for someone who has been taught to fear adults."

"Unless he sees Avery as an outcast like himself. Maybe he senses a kind of bond between them."

"Maybe." Paul acknowledged the possibility with a slow nod. "But he's a very courteous young man. He had to learn that somewhere. And look at his integrity, the way he wouldn't accept payment for cleaning up the yard. All that speaks of someone having a positive influence on him, not a negative one."

Kate took a sip of coffee and leaned back in her chair. "Maybe you're right. But there's *something* there. I just know it."

Paul's eyes crinkled at the corners. "I wouldn't worry about losing your touch, Katie. Between trying to learn more about our young friend and figuring out how your wallet wound up in the Mustang, it sounds to me like God thinks you're doing well enough to entrust you with two mysteries instead of just one."

Kate tipped back her head and laughed. "I much prefer taking them one at a time, thank you."

Heartened by Paul's encouragement, she offered up a new plan. "Next time I see Cody, I'll invite him over for a real meal. You can spend some time talking with him. Maybe he'll open up more to another man."

Kate cleared away the dishes, already planning the menu for the dinner they would share with Cody.

Chapter Twenty-Three

"Look at that glorious sky!" Kate parked her Honda by the front steps of Faith Briar Church and spread her arms wide as if to embrace the clear, dazzling morning. "Spring will be here before we know it."

Paul stepped out into the parking lot, balancing on his moon boot with only minimal difficulty. "You're doing well without the crutches. You're going to be back to normal in no time."

He ducked his head back inside the car and leaned across the seat to give her a kiss. "Thanks for dropping me off. It'll be good to spend some time in my office and start catching up on things."

Kate waved good-bye and watched to be sure he made it to the top of the steps without difficulty before driving off.

The bright day matched her sunny mood. After Paul's reassuring comments the night before, she felt a renewed sense of hope.

God would lead her to the right discovery at the right time. He would make her path straight; all she had to do was put one foot in front of the other and go forth in obedience.

Instead of turning right onto Smoky Mountain Road, she pulled off the road and gave herself a moment to think. A day full of promise stretched out before her. How was she going to use it?

With Paul occupied in his office, she had several hours to call her own before he would need a ride home. If she spent that time in her studio, she could make some major inroads on the fanlight.

On the other hand . . .

Kate tapped her fingers on the steering wheel, considering her options, then she made a left turn onto Smoky Mountain and headed into town.

The doorway to opportunity stood open, and she would strike while the iron was hot.

"Good morning, Skip."

The red-headed deputy blinked when she walked in, then swiveled around in his chair. "Hey, Sheriff. Look who's here."

Sheriff Roberts looked up and set his pen down atop a stack of paperwork. "That's great timing, Kate. I was just getting ready to call you."

Kate stepped across the office to his desk, her heart beating double time. She took a seat in the now-familiar visitor's chair and clasped her hands in her lap. "What is it? Has there been a break in the case?"

Roberts nodded. "Of sorts. I had another conversation with Roland Myers early this morning." He picked up the pen again and twiddled it between his fingers.

"And . . . ?" Kate leaned forward, her pulse pounding. Hadn't she known something special was going to happen today?

"Myers called and told Skip he wanted to talk to me. Said he needed to make a confession."

Kate's breath caught in her throat. "He drove his own car into the diner?"

"That's what I thought at first." Roberts chuckled and tapped his pen against the desk blotter. "It turns out this was a confession of a different kind."

Kate settled back in her seat and waited, trying to mask her impatience.

"Apparently, the Mustang was a gift from his daughter. She knew how much he loved restoring old cars, so she tracked this one down as a special present for his birthday last year."

"Mm-hmm." Kate laced her fingers together to keep from making hurry-up motions.

"Trouble is, Roland's arthritis has gotten so bad, he can barely turn a wrench. Bit by bit, he managed to get the engine working, but he wasn't able to get any farther than that. His daughter told him she'd come out to visit him next month, and he'd been fretting that when she saw the Mustang just sitting there, she'd think he didn't appreciate all the effort she put into getting it for him."

Kate caught her breath. "So he decided to make it disappear so she wouldn't blame him for ignoring her gift?"

"Well . . . not exactly."

Sheriff Roberts rubbed his hand across his chin. "He'd been trying to decide what to do and hadn't been able to come up with a solid solution. The night the car was stolen, he'd been up late worrying about it. He hadn't been in bed very long when he heard someone starting up an engine.

"He said he got up and looked around, but he didn't see anything, so he assumed it was someone out on the road and went back to bed."

"So he didn't drive it away himself." Kate sagged back in her chair and crossed her arms.

"No. When he got up the next morning and saw the car was gone, he put two and two together and realized what he'd heard the night before. Instead of being angry, he felt downright relieved."

The sheriff's mouth widened in a broad grin. "Said he looked at it as divine intervention."

Kate leaned forward again. "And that's why he didn't report the car as stolen?"

"That's it." Sheriff Roberts threw back his head and laughed. "He knew he'd have to call it in eventually, but he thought if he waited long enough, he could give the thief time to get out of town, or preferably out of state. That way, he might never get it back. And that would have been just fine with him. It was insured anyway."

Kate waited for more, but he had apparently finished his story. "That's it?"

The sheriff rolled his pen between his palms and nodded. "I guess it was eating at his conscience, knowing he hadn't been completely honest with me before."

He tossed the pen onto the desktop and stretched his arms over his head. "It doesn't change the situation as far as finding out who took the car, but I thought you'd like to know."

Kate held out her hands, palms up. "What

does that mean as far as the investigation is concerned?"

The sheriff shrugged. "If nothing changes, we're at a standstill. There really isn't much to go on . . . unless we get a better confession than Roland's."

Back in her Honda, Kate debated what to do next. Her studio beckoned, but she couldn't shake off the feeling that this day held significance and she ought to be doing something more about finding out who stole the Mustang.

Roland Myers' "confession" didn't do a thing except take him off the list of suspects, which was already pitifully short.

Her frustration mounted. It seemed like every clue only led to yet another dead end. What was she supposed to do now?

"Start at the beginning." She could almost hear Livvy's cheerful voice.

But where did it all begin? Kate closed her eyes and went back to the night LuAnne's frantic phone call turned her life upside down.

Everything started with the chain of events connected with Roland Myers' stolen Mustang.

Kate nodded slowly. If she were to begin at the beginning, she needed to backtrack to that point. There had to be something everyone, including her, had missed.

She concentrated, picturing the car-littered property in her mind and wondering what it could tell her.

This won't work. Kate shook her head and reached for the ignition. She would have to take another look in person and see it for herself.

She put the Honda into gear and retraced her route to the church and continued east on Mountain Laurel Road. As she drove, she thought back to the night of the crash, trying to put herself into the mind of the thief.

"If I were the one stealing that Mustang, how would I have done it?" she mused. "I wouldn't have gone strolling straight up to Roland Myers' front door, that's for sure."

Instead of turning into Myers' driveway, she drove past it to where a dirt track led off into a wooded area. She turned off the road and found a clear area to one side of the track where she could park her Honda.

With a feeling she was somehow making progress, she got out, locked the car, and pocketed the keys. Now what?

A path led off the track, and Kate followed it into the woods behind Roland Myers' place. Several yards into the thick stand of trees, she halted, wondering whose property she was on. Did Myers' holdings extend back that far? And if they did, what would he say if he caught her poking around in his woods? Suddenly doubting the wisdom of this course of action, she glanced around.

No, she didn't see any signs. Nothing posted to warn trespassers away. Taking heart, she pressed on.

Dead leaves crackled underfoot as she slipped from tree to tree, feeling like a cross between a sneak thief and Daniel Boone. She stepped carefully, not wanting to become entangled in the undergrowth, and tried to put herself in the role of someone about to steal a car.

The thief would have been coming through here at night . . .

A vine snagged her ankle, and she stopped to shake it loose. No, that idea wouldn't work. She couldn't imagine trying to negotiate this snarl of vegetation in the dark, and a flashlight would have given away the thief's position.

She continued walking, turning details over in her mind. If the sheriff was right, and some transient was responsible, what would have brought him clear out here? And why would he have been doing this at night?

The answer to that last question was easy:

he didn't want to be seen. But that posed another problem: how would he spot the Mustang in the dark and know it was there, available for the taking?

He didn't.

The sudden knowledge brought her up short. She stumbled to an abrupt halt, just in time to see the wire fence before her stretching back into the trees on either side.

Kate rested her hand on a fence post while she pursued this new line of thought. He hadn't come across the car by accident.

He'd already seen the Mustang and marked its location. Since no one in his right mind would try navigating this thicket in the dark, he must have come in earlier and waited for night to fall.

But where? Kate felt her pulse race. Surely she was on the right track at last.

She studied the fence that blocked her progress. It stretched out of sight in either direction, with no apparent break. But closer examination showed where the wire was stretched in several places. Others had used those spots as crossing points in the past.

Thankful she had chosen to wear an older pair of slacks, Kate pushed down on the top wire and swung her leg over.

On the other side, the woods were still

thick. She continued traveling in what she hoped would turn out to be the direction of Roland Myers' yard.

Farther in, the brush and trees grew more sparse until they thinned out at the edge of a clearing. A grassy slope lay before her. Down below, Kate could see the edges of Myers' yard, with the spot where the Mustang had sat in clear view.

Kate gazed down upon the peaceful scene, thinking back to the night of the car crash. It had been cold. She remembered shivering on their way to the diner, even with the protection of her heavy sweater.

If she had been up on this hill, she would have wanted to be protected from the weather as well as from the view.

She looked around for a likely spot. Most of the brush and trees offered little cover, having shed their leafy coats the previous fall. But up ahead in that stand of young pines . . .

That was the spot. It had to be. She could see it all in her mind's eye — the would-be car thief slipping across the ground like a furtive shadow, taking refuge in the little grove, then waiting patiently until darkness had settled in and he felt safe to make his move.

Kate studied the cluster of pines from

where she stood, her certainty rising with each passing moment. No better place existed within her range of vision. The trunks and branches would help cut the wind as well as screen the view, thus giving the unseen watcher a perfect place to hide.

She looked down at the ground, hoping to see some telltale mark of the thief's passage, but to no avail. The passage of time and the ravages of the storm had erased whatever sign there might have been.

Nothing seemed to stir around the buildings below. Kate watched a moment longer to make sure she was unobserved, then she crouched low and darted across the dry grass.

Ducking into the shelter of the pines, she braced herself against one of the slender trunks while she caught her breath. From this vantage point, she commanded a surprisingly clear view of Roland Myers' house.

Yes! Elated by this confirmation of her theory, Kate took a long, careful look around her hiding place.

The pines enclosed an area about ten feet square. She stepped to the edge closest to the clearing below and nodded. This is where she would have waited, if she had been the one here that night.

Obviously the actual thief had been of the

same opinion. Here, where the interlaced branches had protected the ground from the effects of the storm, the grass had been matted down, as if someone had crouched at the base of the trees for some time.

Kate sat down, testing the spot. Yes, this was it. She could feel it in her bones. She jumped up again, wishing she could let out a loud Texas whoop.

Paul was right. She hadn't lost her sleuthing ability after all. She had found the very spot where the thief had waited to strike. Now all she needed to do was . . .

What could she do? Exciting as it was, her discovery didn't lead her one step closer to identifying the culprit.

Kate walked in a tight circle, shaking her head. This wasn't the way it was supposed to work. She had come so far; there *had* to be something here, some evidence that would further her investigation.

Sherlock would have pointed out a telling clue to Watson without batting an eye — a strand of red hair caught in the bark of one of the pines, perhaps.

If this had been an old, hard-boiled detective story, the hero would not only have discovered the spot where the culprit had waited, but a pawn-shop ticket or the distinctive print of a boot heel as well, evidence enough to put the criminal away for years.

She, on the other hand, had . . . nothing. No pawn ticket, no footprint, not a single thing to show for all her efforts. She covered her face with her hands, trying to fight off her rising sense of failure.

At least she was starting to get inside the thief's head a bit and understand the way he thought. He was patient, she had learned that much. Not everyone would have been willing to huddle outdoors on a cold night, waiting for the right moment to drive off with someone else's car.

But why would he have done it at all?

No matter how she looked at the problem, that stumbling block refused to go away. Why go to all the trouble of stealing a car, only to crash it into the diner? *And how did he get hold of my wallet?*

Kate turned and examined the bark of the trees one by one. No strands of hair of any description.

She dropped to her hands and knees and checked around the base of the trunks. Except for the depression in the grass, no sign remained of the thief's presence.

A mental image flashed into her mind of the picture she must be making, crawling around in the grass. *I hope no one can see me. They really will think I'm crazy. Or that I've come back here to steal another car.*

She pushed herself to her feet and dusted off her slacks. Her arthritic knee complained at the treatment, and she shifted her weight to the other leg to give it some relief.

"This isn't the way it's supposed to work." She spoke the thought out loud.

She had followed both her instincts and the clues at hand. By rights she should have discovered the clue needed to break the case wide open. Instead she had run headlong into yet another dead end.

Where was the final clue that would lead her to the culprit?

Give it up, Kate. You've wasted enough time out here. Blinking back tears, she turned her back on the stakeout site. Time to get back to the studio and do something productive.

She retraced her steps, keeping the group of pines between her and Myers' clearing. No point advertising her fruitless search. She started for the line of trees, then stopped when something tugged at her ankle.

Looking down, she saw the hem of her slacks had caught in a small thorn bush. She bent over to pull the fabric free before it tore. The bush proved tougher than she expected, so she knelt to work the fabric loose.

The tiny branch gave way with a snap. Ready to push herself upright, Kate looked down by her hand and saw a crumpled wad of paper tangled in the thorns.

She pulled it loose, a stubborn whisper of optimism telling her it might prove to be a clue after all.

When she opened it and smoothed out its creases, her heart sank. Only a candy wrapper. Paul's favorite brand.

She tucked the bit of litter in the pocket of her Windbreaker. It might not have any significance to speak of, but it was the only thing resembling a lead she had at the moment.

And it was just as well she found it rather than someone else. The way local minds were working, that might be enough evidence for them to try to pin the Mustang theft on Paul.

Or maybe the two of them together. Kate made her way back to the fence crossing and started up the path toward her Honda.

I can see the headlines now: PASTOR OF FAITH BRIAR CHURCH AND HIS WIFE HEAD LOCAL CAR-THEFT RING.

Kate kicked at a small rock and sent it skittering away into the undergrowth.

"That's us," she muttered. "The Bonnie and Clyde of Copper Mill."

Chapter Twenty-Four

There was one positive thing to be said for running out of leads to follow, Kate thought. It had given her the time she needed to throw herself back into her stained-glass project.

She spread a sheet of double-thick corrugated cardboard across her workbench and laid the fanlight on top of it with tender care. She took a last loving look at her creation before putting another layer of cardboard over it.

The delicate pink of the dogwood blossoms complemented the vibrant yellow of the forsythia. Leaves in varied hues of green wound their way around the flowers. All in all, it had turned out even better than she expected.

She slid the second sheet into place and taped the edges together to hold the fanlight in a cardboard cocoon of protection, glad she had taken several photos of the finished project. She would have to get them up on her Web site soon.

"Need any help?" Paul asked from the doorway.

Kate glanced down at his moon boot. She had gotten so used to doing things for him in the early days of his injury, she had to remind herself how well he was able to manage now.

"Are you up to it? I can handle it myself if you're not."

Paul flexed his muscles and struck a Charles Atlas pose. "You mean carrying that out to the car? Piece of cake."

Kate hovered anxiously as he lifted the package. "Just make sure this doesn't wind up in pieces." She followed him out to the garage and opened the car door so he could lay the parcel on the backseat.

"Thanks, honey." She gave him a peck on the cheek. "I'll be back soon."

"Take your time. And do something nice for yourself while you're at it. I'm doing fine on my own these days, and you've been working way too hard. You need to take a break."

With the fanlight delivered and Steve's exclamations of approval ringing in her ears, she stood on the sidewalk in front of Smith

Street Gifts, reveling in the sense of accomplishment of a job well done.

She tucked her hands inside the pockets of her Windbreaker and leaned back against the building. If only the other issues in her life could be resolved so easily.

Her fingers wrapped around something in her pocket, and she pulled it out to see what it was. Her eyes widened when she saw the candy wrapper she'd found in the little pine grove above Roland Myers' house.

Kate smoothed the wrinkled paper between her fingers. Her only clue, and she didn't even know whether it was a link in the case or merely litter dropped elsewhere and blown about the countryside before becoming entangled in that thorn bush.

A sigh escaped her lips. Paul had told her to take a break and do something nice for herself. The nicest thing she could think of would be to have the Mustang mystery resolved.

Kate studied the wrapper. Was it worth spending her time trying to follow up on this, or would it wind up being another instance of chasing after the wind?

Just how did one go about following up on a candy wrapper, anyway? She could hardly take it over to Town Hall and demand Skip dust it for prints.

She ran her thumb across the label, ideas churning in her mind. Fertilizers could be traced to specific factories. Bullets had lot numbers and could be traced by those.

Was there a way to determine where something as innocent as a candy bar came from?

Kate raised her eyes and looked over the wrapper to the red-brick building located diagonally across the intersection. Maybe a better question was, who did the candy bar go to?

She crossed Smith Street to the southwest corner of the Town Green, then waited for traffic to let up before hurrying across Main Street. When she reached the sidewalk, she nearly turned back. Why did she think she would find any answers at the Mercantile?

Then again, why not? It might well prove to be a wasted effort, but it wouldn't take long to find out. Then she could go on with the rest of her day. At least she would know she had tried.

Inside the Mercantile, she waited until Sam Gorman was free before walking up to him. "Do you have a minute?"

"Sure, Kate." Sam planted his broad hands on his hips in the stance that always reminded her more of a sea captain than a store owner. "What can I do for you?"

Kate held out the crumpled wrapper. "This may sound like a silly question, but is this a popular brand of candy? Do you sell many of these?"

"Heath bars? Not too many." Sam grinned. "In fact, Paul is my best customer for those. He's the main reason I even keep them in stock."

Kate's hopes plummeted. "Okay, thanks. That's what I needed to know." She pocketed the wrinkled paper again.

So much for her so-called lead. If that was one of Paul's candy wrappers, it must have been quite a wind that had carried it clear out to the Myers' place.

From Sam's look of concern, her expression must have betrayed her disappointment. "I'm sorry if that wasn't the answer you were looking for, but I don't know anybody else around here who likes them as much as he does."

"I can think of one," Arlene Jacobs called from the register. "That new kid is as crazy about them as your husband. He comes in here nearly every day to get one."

She leaned back against the register and toyed with a strand of her bleached-blond hair. "You know the kid I mean, Kate. The one who didn't have enough money the other day. You bought him one of these bars yourself."

Kate's mind flashed back to the snack items she'd purchased for Cody: milk, string cheese, and a candy bar . . . She tried to picture the items one by one.

Yes, Arlene was right. It had been a Heath bar.

So what did that mean? Kate closed her eyes and pressed her fingertips against her temples.

Sam's voice filtered through the jumble of thoughts whirling through her mind. "Are you all right, Kate? You need an aspirin or something?"

She shook her head and smiled. "I'm fine. I just need a minute to think." She walked back to the snack aisle and stared at the candy display, trying to organize the fragments of information she'd picked up along the way.

The Heath wrapper had been tangled in a thorn bush near a prime spot for watching Roland Myers' house.

Cody liked Heath bars as much as Paul did.

Cody was a nice boy she truly liked, but he always had an air of hiding something.

Her eyebrows drew together as she remembered the emphatic way Cody had refused to drive Avery's truck.

An image floated into her mind, the sight of the Mustang sitting in the middle of the wreckage at the diner, with no driver in sight.

With startling clarity, the pieces snapped into focus like a view through Eli's stereoscope.

It isn't two mysteries after all; it's only one. I've been looking at the same problem from different angles all along!

Picking up one of the Heath bars, she weighed it in her hand for a moment. Then she strode to the counter and paid for it before she could change her mind. She slipped the candy bar into her pocket and went outside. Maybe a few brisk laps around the Town Green would clear her head and give her time to decide what to do next.

As it turned out, she didn't have the luxury of time to think.

Kate stood in the shelter of the Mercantile's doorway and watched a familiar figure leaning against the clock tower.

I guess you want me to do this now, don't you?

Even in this public setting, the boy maintained his typical air of caution, distancing himself from contact, to all appearances content to enjoy the sunny afternoon alone.

And Kate was about to cast a long shadow over his day.

Gathering her courage, she sent up a quick prayer for wisdom. She looked from side to side to check the traffic, then trotted across Main Street. She could tell the instant Cody recognized her from the ripple of tension that stiffened his slender frame.

Kate picked up her pace, relieved when he didn't dart away. Surely that marked an improvement in their relationship. Hating what she was about to do, she slid her hands into her pockets and balled them into fists as she walked up to him.

"Pretty afternoon, isn't it?" She pulled out the candy bar and held it out to him without waiting for a response.

Cody's eyes lit up at the sight of the snack, and he took it with a grin. "Thanks." He started to peel the paper back. "It's my favorite."

"I know." Kate settled back against the clock tower and hooked her thumbs in her pockets, trying to look as non-threatening as possible.

"Sam says he doesn't sell a lot of them at the Mercantile. Not too many people like them as much as you and my husband."

Cody bit into the treat with every sign of

enjoyment. "I don't know why. I sure enjoy them."

Affecting a casual air, Kate looked across the street in the direction of the diner, where heavy tarps still hid the building from view.

"It sure seems strange to have the diner shut down. I wonder when Loretta is going to let everybody know what she plans to do with the place."

She watched him closely as she went on. "Did you see the damage before they covered up the front of the building?"

Cody swallowed the last bite of candy and wiped his mouth with the back of his hand. Focusing his eyes on the ground, he mumbled, "I heard it was a real mess."

Kate nodded. "They never have figured out who was driving that night. The car that went through the window belonged to a man named Roland Myers. Have you ever met him?"

Cody shook his head and continued staring at the winter-brown grass. "No, I can't say I have."

This was it, her point of no return. Kate took a deep breath. "I was out at his place the other day."

She pulled the wrapper from her pocket and spread it open so he could see it clearly.

"I found this near a group of pine trees on the hill behind his property."

The boy's eyes flared wide, and he took a step backward. He was going to run. Kate could see it in every line of his body.

She started toward him, hand outstretched. Her steps halted at the sound of a cheery voice.

"Afternoon, Missus Hanlon. Who's your friend?"

Cody spun on his heel, then froze when he saw Skip Spencer in his tan uniform. His head shifted from side to side as if sizing up the potential for escape.

Before he could make a choice that would only make matters worse, Kate closed the distance between them and put her hand on his shoulder. "This is Cody, Skip."

She looked up at the boy's pale face. "Cody, this is Deputy Spencer. He works for Sheriff Roberts, and you have my word that they're both fair and honest men. Do you have something you'd like to tell them?"

Kate could feel the tension vibrating through the teen. She held her breath, hoping he wasn't going to force Skip to chase him and bring him in like a fugitive.

To her great relief, his shoulders sagged, and he nodded. "Yeah, I do. I'm tired of hiding."

Chapter Twenty-Five

Sheriff Alan Roberts propped his elbows on his desk and stared at the young man seated across from him without blinking.

Kate scooted the chair she had commandeered closer to Cody's and gave him an encouraging pat on the arm. "It's going to be all right," she promised. "You can tell him the whole story."

Sheriff Roberts cleared his throat and glanced at Skip, who sat off to one side holding a pen poised over the notebook on his lap. Then he looked back at Cody. "Why don't we start at the beginning? You say your name is Cody?"

The boy looked at the floor and shuffled his feet. "Actually, it's Josh. Josh Cannery."

Shock rippled through Kate. *He lied about his name? Have I misjudged him completely?*

She thought of Paul's admonition not to jump to conclusions and decided to listen to the whole story before she made up her mind.

The sheriff nodded. "Okay, Josh, then. Where do you live? You're not from around here, are you?"

"No sir, not really." Josh glanced up quickly, then looked down at the floor again. "I live in Cullowhee, North Carolina, with my mother. I hitchhiked here to look for my dad." He rubbed his hands together and gulped. "But when I got here, I found out he had moved on."

The sheriff eyed him steadily. "Who told you that?"

"I went to the address he used on some old letters my mom had. Nobody there knew anything about him."

Sheriff Roberts fiddled with his desk pen. "What's your father's name?"

"Andrew Cannery."

The sheriff's eyebrows shot up. "Drew Cannery? I knew him well. I never heard anything about a family, though."

Josh shrugged with a nonchalance that might have fooled Kate had she not seen the flash of pain that crossed his face.

"Maybe we didn't matter to him much. He left when I was six, and I haven't seen him since. He didn't know I was coming."

"How about your mother? Did she know?"

"No, sir. I didn't tell her where I was going. She doesn't know where I am."

"Cody!" The name burst out of Kate's mouth before she could stop herself. "I mean . . . Josh. You've been gone how long? She's probably frantic."

Roberts hushed her with a look. "Why don't you give me her phone number? We'll get in touch with her and let her know you're all right."

He scribbled down the number Josh recited, then leaned back in his chair. "As for your dad, the last I heard, he was in Memphis."

Josh's head bobbed up and down. "That's what I found out."

The sheriff's eyes narrowed. "I thought you said no one at the place he was living could tell you anything about him."

"Yeah, that's right. They didn't have a clue, so I used the library's computer to look him up on the Internet."

Kate smiled to herself. That explained Livvy seeing him around the library so often.

"Then we shouldn't have any problem tracing him," Sheriff Roberts said. "But it doesn't sound like he has custody of you, am I right?"

When the boy nodded, Roberts continued.

"Why don't you just wait here with Mrs. Hanlon and Deputy Spencer while I let your mother know what's going on."

He planted his hands on his desk and started to rise, but Kate held out her hand. "Wait, there's more."

"Okay." He lowered himself slowly back into his chair. "I'm listening."

Kate waited. Cody — *no, Josh,* she reminded herself — hung his head and sat with his hands dangling between his knees as if wishing the floor would open up and swallow him.

The silence lengthened. Kate leaned forward and laid her fingers on his forearm. "Just tell him the truth," she said softly. "You'll feel better once you get it all out."

A shudder ran through the boy's slender frame. "Okay, you're probably right."

He drew a deep breath and sat up straight in his chair to look into the sheriff's eyes. "I'm the one who drove the car into the diner."

The sheriff's jaw sagged. Out of the corner of her eye, Kate saw Skip rise halfway out of his chair. Sheriff Roberts recovered his composure first and gestured to Skip, who scrambled to retrieve the notebook that had fallen to the floor.

Roberts stared down at his desk for a moment, then looked straight at Josh. "Tell me what happened."

Having made up his mind to unburden himself, a flood of words flowed from Josh like water from a bursting dam. "I had to get to Memphis to find my dad, but I didn't want to hitchhike any more. I decided that wasn't such a smart idea."

"No kidding." Skip's mutter earned him a raised eyebrow from Sheriff Roberts.

"I thought maybe I could get a bus ticket, but I didn't have enough money for that. I didn't have enough for food, either, and I was really getting hungry."

Kate's lower lip trembled. She knew he hadn't been eating well, but she never dreamed he'd been reduced to such dire straits.

Sheriff Roberts tapped his fingertips together. "It's been a while since you took that car. You must have had a meal or two since then. How'd you manage?"

Josh looked even more miserable, if that were possible. Staring at his lap, he mumbled a response.

The sheriff frowned. "You need to speak up. I didn't catch that."

Josh raised his head and enunciated clearly: "I said, I took her wallet." He turned to Kate, a look of pleading on his face. "I'm sorry. I thought if I could get enough to buy a ticket to Memphis, my dad could pay you back. I didn't think of it as stealing, not really."

Kate held his gaze. "When did you take it? I still haven't figured that out."

"It was while you were talking to that lady in the library. I'd just found my dad's address, and I knew I had to figure out a way to get to him. You were busy talking, and you walked off and left your purse there on the counter. No one else was around, so I just reached in and grabbed the wallet and stuck it under my jacket and took off."

He looked directly at Kate, his eyelids suspiciously pink. "I never did anything like that before in my life, honest. It just about made me sick, and I've felt bad about it ever since." His voice wobbled. "I don't know why you should believe me, but I'm really, really sorry."

The sheriff's face remained impassive. "So you took her wallet and stole the money out of it. What happened to the bus ride to Memphis?"

Josh licked his lips. "There was enough money in there to buy some food, but not enough for a bus ticket. I didn't know what to do then. I knew if I called my mom and told her what I'd done, she'd skin me."

The sheriff's lips tightened. If not for the steely look in his eyes, Kate would have sworn he was fighting a smile.

Josh continued. "I was scared someone might have seen me take Mrs. Hanlon's wallet, so I had to stay out of sight. I wandered around the back roads the rest of the day, trying to get up enough nerve to start walking to Memphis. I must have walked for miles. Then I realized it was almost sunset, so I started looking for a place to hole up for the night. And I found a good one. At least I thought I did."

He paused. Nothing broke the silence except for the sound of Skip's pen scratching away at the notebook.

"Where was that?" Sheriff Roberts prompted.

Josh's voice grew stronger as he went on with his story. "It was back in the woods, way off the road where no one could spot me. There was this nice little clump of pine trees, and I thought it would make a great place to hide. I decided I'd sleep there and get started for Memphis in the morning."

Kate pictured the pine grove again, this time with Josh huddled in the grass, trying to keep warm. "That was a cold night," she commented.

"Yes, ma'am, it was. But the trees helped

keep the wind off me. And I had a candy bar to snack on." He flashed a furtive glance in her direction.

"But it got even colder after the sun went down. I could see this place at the bottom of the hill in the moonlight. It looked like there were a jillion cars sitting around there, so I figured I could crawl inside one of them and stay warm." He shrugged. "Warmer, at least. So I went on down the hill and got inside the Mustang. That's when the idea hit me."

Sheriff Roberts rolled his pen between his fingers. "What idea was that?"

"The idea that if I could get the car started, I could drive myself to Memphis. I was pretty sure there was enough money in the wallet to pay for the gas. And with so many cars lying around, I didn't think anybody was going to miss one. It was more like borrowing than stealing, you know?"

Kate frowned. "Are you old enough to have a driver's license?"

The boy's face turned dark red. "No, ma'am, I'm not. I just kept thinking about it being a faster way to get to my dad and how great it would be to drive a classic like that Mustang."

His eyes lit up, and his face took on an

expression of awe. "Man, that is one sweet car."

The light in his eyes dimmed. "Or it was, anyway." He looked down again and twisted his hands together. "I guess it was a pretty dumb thing to do."

Skip snorted, and Sheriff Roberts wiped his hand across his mouth.

"How did you get it started?" the sheriff asked. "Hot-wire it?"

Josh looked genuinely offended. "No, sir. I don't know how to do that. But I do know people keep spare keys hidden away sometimes. My mom keeps hers in the ash tray, so I looked there first. Then I saw a rubber band wrapped around the visor. My uncle puts his spare key there, so I checked, and there it was."

He shifted in his chair. "I did think hard about what I was going to do, believe it or not. And I had plenty of time to think, because that man who lives there . . ." — the boy's voice took on an aggrieved tone — "well, I thought he never would go to sleep. He must have been watching a late movie or something. It was really late by the time he turned off all his lights. Then I had to wait even longer to give him time to go to sleep."

But not nearly long enough. Kate remembered Roland Myers' comment about hearing the car drive away.

Josh rubbed his palms together. "Like I said, I found the key, and the car started up right away. It was already pointed toward the road, so I just headed down the driveway and kept going. I didn't turn the headlights on until I was sure no one at the house could see me."

Sheriff Roberts propped his elbows on the desk and rested his chin on his fist. "But you didn't exactly make it to Memphis."

"Well, no. You see, Mrs. Hanlon was right. I'm not old enough for a license yet." Another quick glance at Kate. "But I've driven my grandpa's truck around out at his farm. It's an automatic, though. I've never driven a stick shift. It isn't as easy as it looks."

Kate wanted to laugh at his bewildered expression.

"I was doing pretty good until I got into town. Then I thought maybe I ought to shift gears again. It kind of got away from me, and I hit the curb. Next thing I knew, that big window was right in front of me, and there wasn't anything I could do to keep from going through it."

Kate couldn't keep from asking, "Were you hurt?"

"Not then, but I was pretty stiff for the next day or two. The only thing I could think of right then was that I'd really messed up, and I needed to get away."

"A regular one-man crime wave." The barely audible comment came from Skip's part of the room.

"I found a phone booth and used some more of Mrs. Hanlon's money to call the number I found on the Internet." Josh's voice caught. "All I got was a message saying the number wasn't in service. I guess my dad has moved on. Again."

Sheriff Roberts seemed unmoved by his show of emotion. "And after all this, you still didn't leave town. Why?"

Josh threw his arms out wide. "Where could I go? I knew how mad my mom would be if I went home. The best thing I could think of was to stay out of sight except for when I needed to come out and get some food or find a place to get warm. There weren't too many places I could do that, though. The library was okay, because I could get on the computer and try to find out more about my dad. I tried going to one of the basketball games, because I thought it would be a good way to get in out of the cold for a while."

He looked over at Kate and shook his

head. "But I saw you there, so I took off. And after a while, it seemed like no matter where I went, I kept running into you."

The corner of Kate's mouth twisted upward. "Literally, that first time."

"Yeah. Every time I turned around, you were there. I almost thought you'd figured out I took your wallet and were going to get back at me somehow." He gave a shaky laugh. "It was kind of creepy."

"Or maybe God kept bringing us together for a bigger reason."

Josh took a deep breath and held her gaze. "Yeah, maybe. You've been really nice to me when I didn't deserve it. I'll try to find some way to pay you back."

"Is that why you gave back the money we paid you for cleaning up our yard?"

The sheriff shot a sharp glance at her but didn't say anything.

"That's right." Josh nodded eagerly. "It wasn't much, but I thought it might help a little. That and putting the shingles back up on the church with Mr. Griffin."

Sheriff Roberts cleared his throat again. "Where have you been staying all this time? The weather's been too cold for sleeping outdoors."

"Don't I know it." The boy shivered. "I started out sleeping in the church basement the night after the accident."

Kate stared. "At Faith Briar?"

"Yes, ma'am. But I didn't know your husband was the pastor there. I was so busy trying to keep away from you, I wouldn't have gone within a mile of the place if I'd known that."

Kate bit back a smile. "But how did you get in?"

He shrugged. "The door was unlocked the first time. I thought maybe that was something churches did. But just in case, I stuck a little rock in the doorjamb. That way everything looks fine, but the door doesn't close all the way."

Kate made a mental note to remind Paul to double-check the doors before he left the church from here on.

Josh's cheeks bulged as he blew out a puff of air. "You scared the socks off me that time you stopped by, you know."

Kate spread her hands. "Which time?"

"You know, about a week after the crash. I think it was a Saturday. I was down in one of those little rooms off the basement when I heard somebody come in. That really shook me, because I wasn't expecting anybody to come around until Sunday morning."

The light dawned. "Saturday. The day I

went in to clean for Avery. So it was you I heard slipping out the front door?"

Josh bobbed his head up and down. "You nearly caught me that time. I was beginning to think I was jinxed or something."

The sheriff cut in. "So you've been sleeping in the church all this time?"

"No way." The boy's tone left no room for argument. "Not after that. It was too many close calls all at once."

He rubbed the back of his neck. "I found an old barn out on the edge of town. It's a really run-down place. Nobody's living there. I checked first this time."

Kate put her hand to her lips. "You've been sleeping in a barn? In this weather?"

Josh shrugged. "It isn't so bad. I found some old blankets, and I crawl in under a pile of hay. The hardest part has been getting enough to eat . . ."

He trailed off and looked at the sheriff. "I guess I'm in a lot of trouble now, aren't I?"

Sheriff Roberts tapped the end of his pen against his desk and pursed his lips. "Let's see. Petty theft, grand theft auto, reckless endangerment, destruction of property . . ."

Josh sunk lower in his seat as the tally grew.

". . . breaking and entering, trespassing." The sheriff leaned back and regarded the boy thoughtfully. "That's a pretty impressive list of charges already, some of them felonies. And I can probably come up with a few more if I put my mind to it."

Except for his bobbing Adam's apple, Josh could have been made of stone.

The sheriff let the silence stretch out before adding, "I do have some leeway in the matter, but a lot depends on what some other people decide to do about it. Namely, Mrs. Hanlon, Mr. Myers, and Mrs. Sweet."

Chapter Twenty-Six

"And so the sheriff released him into your custody?" Paul helped Kate pick up the last of the serving dishes and carried them to the counter.

Kate waved him back to the table. "Just for tonight. The only alternative was for them to let him sleep in one of the cells. I couldn't do that."

She sank into the chair opposite Paul's and lowered her voice so as not to disturb the exhausted boy stretched out on the fold-out couch in Paul's study. "He needs a good night's sleep, and he wasn't going to get it there."

Paul dropped his tone to match hers. "I didn't want to ask too many questions during dinner. It was obvious he'd already been through the wringer. What I've picked up so far is that he ran away from home and came here looking for his father, then he wrecked the Mustang when he tried to drive it to

Memphis. Right?"

Kate smiled wearily. "That's the short version. We'll save the details for after this is all over."

"Which will be . . . ?"

"Tomorrow around lunchtime, if all goes according to plan. The sheriff got ahold of both Josh's parents. It seems his dad is still in Memphis. They had a storm that knocked out the phone lines for a couple of days, and Josh assumed he had moved when he'd been there all along."

Paul shook his head. "Poor kid."

"His mother agreed to let his dad bring him back home so they could all sit down together and sort things out."

Paul's lips curved. "I have a feeling he'll be glad to have some backup when he faces her after taking off like that."

"I have a feeling you're right." Kate managed a laugh. "She's been beside herself ever since he left, and who can blame her?"

Paul stretched his leg out and leaned down to adjust his moon boot. "It was a foolish thing to do, all right, but I guess we all do some foolish things when we're young."

"Amen to that. But I suspect this particular young man has learned a good bit in the past couple of weeks. I can just about guarantee he'll never be tempted to take something that doesn't belong to him after this. Especially after Sheriff Roberts told him he could have spent the next three years in a juvenile detention center for what he did."

Paul let out a low whistle. "Does he have any idea how fortunate he is that Myers and Loretta chose not to press charges?"

"He does now. He was a very shaken young man by the time it was all said and done." She stifled a giggle. "At least by the time Loretta got through with him. She and LuAnne came down together and read him the riot act. I thought he was ready to break down and cry when Loretta told him he could do her more good by coming back and working off his debt during the next couple of summer vacations than sitting in juvie somewhere. It won't begin to cover what the insurance paid for the damage, but he'll be taking some responsibility for his actions."

Paul grinned. "She'll spoil him to death once she gets over being mad. Does he know that?"

"He will." Kate chuckled. "At least he won't have to worry about being hungry the next time he comes to Copper Mill."

"What about Roland Myers? I get the feeling his reaction may have been a whole different story."

Kate pressed her hand over her mouth to hold back her laughter. "I'll say. He was so relieved to have an excuse not to work on that Mustang, I think he would have pinned a medal on Josh if he'd had one. It wasn't quite the response Sheriff Roberts was expecting."

"And what about you?" Paul reached over and tucked a wayward strand of hair behind her ear. "I assume you didn't press charges against him for stealing your wallet and landing you in the middle of this whole mess."

Kate tilted her head and pressed her cheek against his palm. "Mercy triumphs over judgment," she quoted from one of her favorite verses.

"There's a lot of good in that boy, Paul. We both felt it. More than anything, he needs a father's guidance. I think this will be a turning point in his life."

Paul's eyes took on a tender gleam, and he leaned across the table to touch his lips to hers. "I love you, Katie girl."

"You okay back there, son?" Paul turned and looked over his shoulder at Josh riding in the rear seat of Kate's Honda. "You're jumpier than a jackrabbit at a coyote convention."

Kate peered in the rearview mirror in time to catch sight of the boy's shamefaced grin. "Sorry. I guess I'm just nervous." He resumed his fidgeting, but in a more restrained manner.

Paul turned to look at Josh over the seat back. "I know it's a big moment for you, but it's going to be okay. Just take it one step at a time."

Kate put her left blinker on and turned south down Euclid. "He told the sheriff he'd meet us at the clock tower, so I thought I'd park somewhere by the Town Green. But look! All the parking places are full, every last one of them. What on earth is going on?"

"I have no idea." Paul turned back around and looked out the windshield. "I've never seen it like this on a weekday morning."

He scanned the parking slots as she drove along the east side of the green, then turned right onto Main Street. "Maybe we should try over by the library."

Kate pressed the accelerator. "That's probably our best —"

"Hey, look over there!" Josh scooted forward, pointing between them across the green toward the corner of Smith and Hamilton. "What are all those people doing?"

Kate looked toward the spot he indicated and saw a mob of people coming from every direction, converging on the diner like an army of ants.

Oh no. Not again.

"Over there!" Josh shouted, practically in her ear. "There's a place to park between that blue van and the white truck."

Kate eyed the slot. It was barely wide enough to qualify as a parking space. She took it anyway, trying to leave more room on Paul's side of the car.

She eased her own door open and squeezed out, then ran around the front of the car and motioned to Paul and Josh. "Come on."

The three of them hurried across the green as quickly as Paul could manage with his moon boot. Just as they reached the outer edge of the crowd, Paul grabbed Kate's hand. "Wait. It isn't another demonstration. Look up there."

Kate looked over the heads in front of her and felt as if she'd traveled back to a time before the accident. The tarps were gone, and the building looked just as it did before.

No, not quite. Stretched across the front of the building, a brightly colored banner proclaimed: Welcome to Our Grand Reopening!

Tears stung Kate's eyes. She dashed them away, then squeezed Paul's arm. "I don't believe them. Neither Loretta nor LuAnne said a word about this yesterday."

A familiar voice rang out. "May I have your attention!"

Kate craned her neck and saw Loretta Sweet, apparently standing on some kind of platform that put her in view of the whole crowd.

The hum of voices diminished, then quieted altogether.

Loretta cleared her throat. "I've been in this town a long time, and I've spent a lot of hours back in that old kitchen. When the accident took out the dining area, I really wondered if this wasn't an opportunity to turn lemons into lemonade . . . in other words, to grab the cash from the insurance and run off to Florida and live happily ever after. But the loyalty of my customers made me rethink that idea — even if some of you carried it a little too far." Her pointed glances brought ripples of nervous laughter from various spots in the crowd.

"Anyway, the good news is, I've decided to stay. The Country Diner has been a fixture in Copper Mill for a good many years, and it's going to continue to be just that as long as I'm around."

She raised both arms into the air. "So thank you all for coming out today. We're going to reopen the doors now, and we want to invite you inside for a look at the all-new Country Diner!"

Cheers erupted, and the mass of people started moving forward. Kate looked hopefully at Paul, but he shook his head.

"There's no way we'd be able to move around inside with all those people. Let's wait until after Josh's dad comes. Things should thin out by then."

They stood back in a little knot while jubilant customers descended on the diner. Kate leaned against Paul. "I'm glad she decided not to take the money and run."

"Me too. Copper Mill just wouldn't have been the same without —"

"Pastor?"

They turned at the sound of the voice behind them. Avery Griffin stood next to Josh, shuffling his feet.

"I'm glad I ran into you," he said. "I wanted to tell you good-bye."

Paul's jaw dropped. "What's going on? Did I miss something?"

Avery smiled and shook his head. "I made up my mind a couple of days ago, and I want to do this before I lose my nerve."

"You're leaving?" Kate sputtered. "But why?"

Avery looked away, then back at Paul. "I've learned a lot workin' for you at the church. The faith you had in me made me have faith in myself. And that helped me prove to myself that I can clean up my act and stay sober."

Joy shone in the broad smile that creased his cheeks. "It's a good feelin', I can tell you that. I know you've taken some flak for hiring me. No one's ever stood by me like that before, and I want you to know how much I appreciate it."

Josh's face scrunched up. "I don't get it. If things are going so great, why do you want to take off? Running away doesn't solve anything."

When all three adults stared at him, he ducked his head and kicked at the grass. "Well, it doesn't," he mumbled. "Believe me, I ought to know."

Avery clapped the boy on the back. "You're right about that, and it's a good lesson to learn." He turned back to Paul. "I know I can stay on the straight and narrow, but most people around here aren't ever gonna let me forget my past. I want to move on and make a new start somewhere else."

Paul hooked his thumbs in his pockets and

angled his head to one side. "I understand, and I can't say I blame you. Keep in touch, will you? We'll be praying for you."

Paul extended his hand. "You're a good man, Avery. It's been a pleasure knowing you."

Avery started to speak, then he clamped his lips together and gripped Paul's hand in a firm handshake. He looked at Kate next. "Missus Hanlon, you've been real good to me too. I'll never forget the way you and LuAnne came out to check on me when I was sick."

Kate could see his chin tremble ever so slightly when he turned and held out his hand to Josh.

Instead of responding, Josh stared over Avery's shoulder with a frozen expression on his face.

"That's him. That's my dad. Even after ten years, I'd know him anywhere."

Chapter Twenty-Seven

Kate followed the direction of Josh's gaze and saw a lanky man in his late thirties walking their way.

She stepped back to let her young friend move past her, then linked her fingers in Paul's. They waited until Josh had nearly reached his father before walking in their direction.

Both Josh and his dad stopped when a few feet still separated them. Even from a distance, Kate could see the similarity between the two. The man's features showed her exactly how his son would look in twenty years or so.

"Josh?" A smile creased Drew Cannery's face, though he didn't move to close the gap between them.

Kate could read the underlying emotions as easily as if they had been printed on a page. Both joy and uncertainty warred within him.

Her gaze switched back to Josh, wondering what he felt now that his search had ended. He had told them he had been trying to find his father, but he'd never said why.

As far as Kate could recall, he never specified whether he wanted to reconnect and fill an empty spot in his life or confront the man who had abandoned his family all those years ago.

She clung to Paul's fingers as they watched the little drama play out before them.

"You've grown into a fine young man." The muscles in Drew's jaw knotted while he waited for an answer.

Josh didn't seem to know whether he felt more like a young man or a child at that moment. He started to raise both arms, then let them fall back to his sides.

Drew's gaze dropped to Josh's shoulders, and a faint smile curved his lips. "Is that my old jacket?"

"Yeah. Mom let me have it after you left. I always figured I'd come find you once I grew into it." The boy's voice cracked. "It's all I had left of you."

Kate could see the tears welling up in Drew Cannery's eyes. He held out his arms and stepped forward. Josh hesitated only an instant before flinging himself into his father's embrace.

"I'm sorry, son. I'm so sorry." Drew's face twisted, and he looked like he was trying to hold back a flood of emotions that had been held at bay for the past decade.

"I thought it was for the best. Our problems — your mother's and mine — shouldn't have hurt you. I thought it was best to move on and let you forget about me."

Josh's shoulders heaved. "How was I supposed to forget you? You're my dad."

Kate turned her face against Paul's shoulder to recover her own composure. He held her close and pressed a handkerchief into her hand. She used it to wipe her eyes, then returned it to him with a grateful smile.

"I'm sorry, son. I should have known. I've missed out on so much of your life." Drew moved back and dashed the tears from his face with the back of his hand. "But I'm not going to miss any more. We'll work something out, the three of us. I promise."

"That sounds good." Josh's voice was just as husky as his father's. He took a deep breath and glanced around as if he had just remembered they were in a public place. He turned and pointed to Kate and Paul.

"These are the Hanlons. They're the ones I stayed with last night."

Drew draped his arm over Josh's shoulders and stepped forward. "Thanks for watching over my boy."

Paul smiled. "We were glad to have him with us, but it was God who did the watching while he's been here."

"Kate? Kate Hanlon!" LuAnne Matthews scurried across the street and bustled over to them. She pressed her hand against her heaving chest until she recovered enough breath to speak.

"I thought I saw you out here. Come on inside and join the celebration."

LuAnne made little shooing motions with her hands. "Come on, I can't stay too long. Loretta needs me back inside." She waved her arms as if to herd them ahead of her, then she stopped in her tracks, and her jaw dropped.

"Drew Cannery! I haven't seen you in ages." She looked at Josh, then at Drew, then back to Josh again and nodded knowingly. "I should have realized who you are, darlin'. Same eyes, same mouth, same build; you two are as alike as two peas in a pod."

Pointing toward the diner, she said, "Both of you oughtta come in as well. We're having an open house, and Loretta has gone all out on little cakes and fancy sandwiches."

She dropped a broad wink at Josh. "You

might consider coming in the door this time. We've decided not to stick with the drive-through concept."

Drew gave his son a long look. "You feel comfortable going in there, after what happened?"

Josh grinned. "It's going to be okay, Dad. The owner's a nice lady. I'll fill you in later."

"On that and a whole lot more, I hope." Drew clapped him on the shoulder and started across the street toward the diner. "We have a lot of catching up to do."

Kate and Paul trailed behind them. Paul looped his arm around Kate's waist. "It looks like a happy ending for Josh and his dad."

Kate nodded, her heart brimming with gratitude for the way things had turned out. "I'm sure they still have some rough roads ahead, but at least they're on the right track."

She tugged at Paul. "Come on! I can't wait to see what Loretta has done inside. I wonder what she meant by the 'all-new' Country Diner?"

Lagging behind a bit, Paul protested. "I'm not sure I want to find out. I liked the place just the way it was."

"As hush-hush as Loretta kept this whole project, it's anybody's guess. But my curiosity is in high gear. Let's go!"

Paul laughed and let her coax him inside.

"Oh my." Kate pressed close to Paul, trying to keep the jostling crowd from making him lose his balance.

She pivoted in a circle to get a view of the whole interior. "Are you seeing what I'm seeing?"

Paul nodded, his jaw slack. "I see it, but I don't believe it."

"I don't either." Kate finished her circuit and looked up at him incredulously. "Everything looks just like it did before."

A slow grin spread over Paul's face. "Yeah. It feels like home. She didn't change a thing."

It was true. Kate felt like she had stepped back in time. She ticked off a mental checklist as she looked around. It was all there, just as it had been before — the blue gingham curtains, the blue-topped tables, the booths along the walls. The new counter was slightly longer and Loretta had added a few more tables, but aside from the smell of paint, it was exactly the same. Kate could see J. B. Packer behind the stove through the little service window to the kitchen.

Across the room, she saw LuAnne waving at them and pointing to a table.

They threaded their way through the excited, laughing throng. In a booth on the opposite wall, Josh and his dad sat in deep conversation, oblivious to all the commotion going on around them.

LuAnne motioned for them to sit when they reached the table. "Let me bring you a couple plates of goodies. We'll go back to the regular menu tomorrow, but we knew there would be too much of a crowd today for business as usual."

She returned a few minutes later carrying plates piled high with a tempting variety of finger foods. Loretta trailed along behind her.

Kate tried to mask her delight long enough to give each of them a stern look. "Why didn't the two of you say something when I saw you at the sheriff's office yesterday? I had no idea anything like this was going on."

LuAnne set the plates down and wiped her hands on her apron. "I didn't know it myself until a few days ago, when Loretta swore me to secrecy. I almost let it slip a few times, but I managed not to say anything. We didn't even let J.B. know until last night. You never saw a man look happier to be going back to work than he did."

She looked toward the ceiling and shook her head. "Keeping that secret was one of the hardest things I ever did. You know how I like to talk."

Paul grinned up at Loretta. "So this is what you've been doing behind the tarps all this time?"

"Yep." If Loretta had been a cat, Kate would have expected to see canary feathers sticking out of her mouth. "My nephew is a contractor up in Pine Ridge. He brought his crew down, and they've been working overtime. I knew no one in this town would be able to keep it under wraps."

"I'm surprised you kept it exactly the same, though," Kate said. "I can't see any changes except for everything looking fresh and new."

"People liked it the way it was. If it ain't broke, don't fix it. That's my motto." Loretta grinned. "The only real difference is in the kitchen. I had all new equipment put in there so it's up to date. It ought to make my job back there a lot easier."

She beamed at the noisy crowd filling the diner. "When all is said and done, having that car drive in here turned out to be a blessing in disguise. The place has needed sprucing up for a long time."

"But why all the secrecy?" Paul asked. "And why didn't you let anyone know you were reopening today?"

Loretta pulled up a chair and sat down, folding her arms on the table. "I love running this place, but it's hard work all the same. When I found out what the insurance settlement would be, retirement sounded like a pretty good idea. Then I thought maybe I'd rebuild the restaurant, put in a lot of fancy doodads, and sell it. That would have given me even more to retire on."

Loretta shrugged. "People kept saying how much they wanted the diner back, and me with it, but I had to see for myself how serious they were before I committed to staying here instead of selling."

"I still don't understand why you didn't tell anybody," Kate said. "As much as people were pressuring you to reopen, I'd think you would have wanted to let everybody know. At least put an ad in the *Chronicle*, or something like that." She waved as the Jenner family walked in and settled into a booth.

"They still showed up, though, didn't they?" Loretta's cat-with-a-canary smile returned. "I've been reading a bunch of articles on public relations. They say word of mouth is the best advertising, so I decided I'd just hang the banner up and see what happened."

She shrugged. "I didn't want folks to

come just because they cut a coupon out of the paper and wanted a meal at half price. I wanted them to be here because they love the place as much as I do."

Paul scooted his chair out of the way of a family trying to reach a nearby table. "I have to admit it looks like it worked."

"I'll say it did!" Loretta's triumphant laugh rang out through the diner. "Somebody saw the banner and called their friends, then they called some others, and things just took off from there."

She folded her arms across her chest and gave a satisfied nod. "In PR terms, this is what we call 'buzz.' "

Paul laughed. "They're glad to have you back, Loretta. No doubt about that."

Kate let her gaze wander around the room to the people she had grown to love. Word must have spread about the truth of the car's driver as quickly as it had about the diner's reopening, for the faces turned her way were friendly, open, accepting.

Faces. Their ability to reflect what lay within a person's heart had always fascinated Kate.

Many of the faces gathered in that room had darkened with suspicion when she and Paul first arrived, not sure they could trust the city slickers who left their San Antonio church to come minister to the little flock on the banks of Copper Mill Creek.

She and Paul had wondered both then and later whether they had made a mistake in coming, if they'd ever be accepted in this tight-knit community.

But God didn't make mistakes. The joyful certainty unfolded in Kate's heart like spring buds bursting into full bloom.

He knew exactly what he was doing. And he had walked beside her every step of the way through another adventure in Copper Mill.

ABOUT THE AUTHOR

Carol Cox is the author of more than twenty novels and novellas. Her nonwriting time is devoted to being a pastor's wife, a homeschool mom and, recently, a grandmother. Carol makes her home with her husband and young daughter in northern Arizona, where the deer and the antelope really do play — often within view of the family's front porch. To learn more about Carol and her books, visit www.CarolCoxBooks.com.

The employees of Thorndike Press hope you have enjoyed this Large Print book. All our Large Print titles are designed for easy reading, and all our books are made to last. Other Thorndike Press books are available at your library, through selected bookstores, or directly from us.

For information about titles, please call:

(800) 223-1244

or visit our Web site at:

http://gale.cengage.com/thorndike

To share your comments, please write:

Publisher
Thorndike Press
295 Kennedy Memorial Drive
Waterville, ME 04901

Guideposts magazine and the annual devotional book *Daily Guideposts* are available in large-print editions by contacting:

Guideposts Customer Service
P.O. Box 5815
Harlan, IA 51593
www.guideposts.org
1-800-431-2344